Anything Could Happen

Anything

Could Happen

WILL WALTON

The publisher does not have any control over and does not assume any responsibility for author or third-party websites or their content.

This book is a work of fiction. Names, characters, places, and incidents are either the product of the author's imagination or are used fictitiously, and any resemblance to actual persons, living or dead, business establishments, events, or locales is entirely coincidental.

ISBN 978-1-338-03249-9

10 9 8 7 6 5 4 3 2 1   16 17 18 19 20

Printed in the U.S.A.   40
First printing 2016

Book design by Elizabeth B. Parisi

For Mom and Dad, who carry me in

one

Let me tell you about the first time I knew for sure I was in love with Matt Gooby.

We were in church. Reverend Greene was winding down her annual September 11th sermon, saying, "Hold fast to that which is good," her blond bouffant wobbling as she leaned toward the congregation with a pleading sincerity. "Our eternal home," she said, "is really only just half a step away from any of us. And the moment when it comes time to take that half step—we can't know when, obviously—but chances are it might not be pretty. Chances are the timing won't *feel* right. And, folks"—I loved that she addressed us all like that—"I'm just trying to be straight with you, but the time to hold fast to that which is good is now. It wasn't yesterday. It's not nine years from now. It's not when we retire. Or when we graduate. It is now. That which is good is now."

Everyone was dead quiet then. Just a few creaks coming up from the saggy wooden pews. I tried not to look around because I got the sense that maybe some people were crying.

"So take the hand of the person next to you." Reverend Greene smiled. "And grip down. Go on, grip down on them hard—it won't hurt 'em!"

A couple of chuckles throughout the sanctuary, the tension slightly cut. Mom, on my right, grabbed my hand so hard my knuckles shot off a popping sound. Then she leaned in close and whispered, "I love you so much, my Tretch." When she pulled back there was some wet left on my face, and I just thought, *Good grief, Mom, don't cry*, and shrugged my shoulder to my cheek to brush it off, planning to make a face at Matt or roll my eyes while I did. Something to show him that I was, you know, over it.

But when I glanced over at him I saw that his eyes were shut *so* tight, like he was determined not to open them. And his left hand was gripping the edge of the pew so hard. *Hold fast*, I thought, and then, *Hold fast because life is fast*, which seemed like a logical conclusion.

That's when he slid his right hand along the edge of the seat, found mine, and squeezed. It sent this gentle buzzing feeling right up the back of my neck, and with it not a *complete* thought yet, but the *essence* of a thought, the kind that gets lost between bigger, louder thoughts. The kind of thought that's barely louder than a feeling itself.

His thumb slid into the pocket of my hand. Or maybe it clamped down over my throat, square over the Adam's apple. Or maybe it plunged straight into my chest. I don't know. Reverend Greene was inviting us now to close our eyes for a moment and meditate, and like that was the cue, Mom's hand let go, and all around me was the dull sound of hands dropping or being dropped.

Matt's hand did not let go.

I closed my eyes. I felt everyone else on one side of me—my mom, my dad, and my brother. And on the other side—Matt, whose smile with the gap in it made me want to hug not just him but his entire world close to me, who somehow in that moment made me believe that bringing both his and my worlds together could happen, like there wouldn't be any struggle involved.

You're in love, Tretch—the thought came to me as Reverend Greene called the meditation to an end, saying, "Oh Lord God, please help us to hold fast to that which is good—which is everything—in this lifetime." When she said, "Amen," I let go of his hand. Physically, I mean, I let go of his hand.

The rest of me held on.

two

Now it's over three months later, nearing the end of December.

I'm still holding. On to what, I'm not entirely sure.

Today in school, during last-period math, a note gets passed around.

It says *Tretch Farm + Matt Gooby* inside a little heart.

Matt and I just kind of shrug it off. The joke is old. It doesn't really matter to us, not even when we hear snickering, not even when Mrs. Cook intercepts the note from Spencer Finch's clenched hand at the front of the classroom.

Mrs. Cook asks me to stay behind after class. She doesn't ask Matt because, like most everyone, she assumes Matt is gay because he has two gay dads. (He isn't.) She also believes I'm some hero for being his friend, I think.

"Now, Tretch," she says. She has on these weird puffed sleeves under a pair of corduroy overalls. "I know how something like this must feel." She scratches a red spot on her arm. "But I think this kind of joking has gone on long enough."

You're right, I think. *It has.*

"You're a good kid who doesn't deserve to have these kind of"—she moves the scratching to her chin—"*accusations* being hurled at you." She sends spit flying with her enunciation of "accusations," and I'm hit.

"I know it must upset you," she says.

Well, not that badly, I think, wiping my face.

"And it must upset your parents."

It would, I guess, if they knew.

"So I'd be willing to get to the bottom of this if you wanted." She holds up the note and I recognize the handwriting immediately. There's no need to get to the bottom of anything.

"Bobby Handel," I say. "That's Bobby Handel's handwriting."

Mrs. Cook's eyes get big. Her nostrils flare.

"But don't say anything," I plead. "Please."

"But, Tretch, I want to—"

"I know you want to help, Mrs. Cook. But, honestly, Bobby Handel's dad and my dad—"

"Are business partners. I know." She nods sympathetically.

"Right," I say. "So I just try to keep the peace."

"But, Tretch, the school has a zero tolerance policy for bullying."

"I *know*, I know." I hold up my hand. "But it's not really *bullying*, Mrs. Cook. You know?"

Mrs. Cook puffs out her cheeks, mimicking her sleeves. Then she sighs. "I guess, if you say so."

"Plus," I say, "it's winter break now. Nobody's even gonna remember this little note fiasco when we get back."

She nods, then smiles. "Well, tell your family I said have a merry Christmas, okay?"

"Sure thing, Mrs. Cook."

"Oh, and your grandparents, too!"

"Oh, I will." I stand up and pull the desk into place.

"Will you be seeing them over break? Your grandparents?"

I turn around again and force a big smile. "Yes, ma'am. I'll be sure to tell 'em for ya." My backpack rests lightly against my shoulder, all my textbooks stowed in my locker for the break. I give Mrs. Cook a final wave, and I am outta there.

Matt is waiting on me in the hallway when I emerge. I pretend not to see and walk right into him, nudging him against the water fountain.

"Whoops, *sorry*," I say, pressing a little closer before pulling away. Just because, in that moment, I can.

"Hey, hey, *what's the big idea?*" He lands me a flat tire on the back of my sneaker, so I have to stop and readjust. "What'd the Cookster say? She ask you about the note?"

"Yeah. She wanted to do something about it. I told her no harm, no foul."

"Bobby Handel write it?"

"Yessir."

Matt cracks a smile. "Tretch Farm," he says. "Sticking up for bullies since the playground days."

"Like a champ." I pump my fist in the air. We're walking down the hallway toward the exit, past rusted lockers and piles of discarded papers. "Matt, in approximately nine steps we will be freed from this place for an entire winter break. How does that make you feel?"

"It makes me feel—" He takes one giant step forward and kneels in a runner's pose. "*Pyow!*" He lights off in a dead sprint, barreling through the double doors of Warmouth High. As soon as he's down the front steps, he turns around and gives the building the middle finger. Two middle fingers, actually.

"Matt!" I say.

"School's out, baby!" he cries.

Mom always says, when she hears someone talking smack about the Goobys or about gay marriage being legalized and stuff, "What people do in the privacy of their own home doesn't bother me." But talking about the Goobys still makes her kind of uneasy, I can tell. That's how I've been Matt Gooby's best friend for a year and a half now without ever going over to his house.

As if staying away from Matt's dads could stop me from being who I am.

I mean, it's a little too late for that.

A lot of the time, I try to picture the worst thing that could happen, if the word got out about me. Like the whole town of Warmouth exploding in a bright red fiery flame caused by rioting civilians who've finally discovered my big gay secret. Or my family might implode—like a submarine when it gets too deep and the pressure's too high.

I imagine telling them. I play the scene out in my mind. We'll be in our living room, hardwood with the Chinese-print throw rug, the record player, the TV, and the coffee table (minus the glass vase I knocked over that time I was practicing my dance moves). Mom and Dad will be there, and Joe, too.

"Mom and Dad, I *am*—" I will say to them.

Then I'll flake out. "—so hungry. Is there anything to eat?"

"Sure, Tretch. Check the fridge. I just bought some turkey." Mom will be wearing her turtleneck, the color of darkened Pepto-Bismol, Dad his hunting jacket. I will look at its camo print and hear the sound of duck calls in my ear and feel guilty. Mom will be sitting on the couch, Dad in his easy chair. I won't focus in on either of them, but instead on the blank spot on the coffee table where the glass vase once sat. Mom's never noticed it missing. Dad neither. I've always thought that was weird.

"Tretch, is something wrong?" Mom will ask.

"Yes," I'll say. "There's something I'm not telling you."

"What, Tretch?" Dad will lean forward in his seat. "What is it?"

"I practice dance moves when you guys leave the house. I choreograph dances as a hobby."

"Oh," Dad will say. "So that's all that thumping I hear coming from your room sometimes."

"Once when I was practicing I knocked over the vase that used to sit right there on the coffee table."

"Oh." Mom will shrug. "We've noticed that was gone for a while."

"We just assumed you or Joe got hard up for cash and sold the thing on eBay." Dad will chuckle. "It didn't mean a thing anyway, just a cheap wedding present."

"I'm gay," I'll say.

They'll stare blankly. And then I'll hear a *pop!* And another. The walls will shake and then stop, and I'll realize— we're in the submarine, and the pressure has gotten too great. The walls are going to cave in and crush us. We are going to die. "*What's happening?*" Joe cries. A window breaks: one, two, then three. "Save yourselves!" I shout to Mom and Dad and Joe, and they obey, jumping out the windows as the walls come straight at me.

Yes, I'll think dramatically, *it's better this way.*

But, truthfully, it wouldn't happen like that.

Nope.

Truthfully, Mom, Dad, and Joe would willingly go down with me. They would go down with me any day. No matter what I do, or say, or whatever person I could be, or might be, or am. That's what makes it so hard to tell them. That they'll suffer it all for me. The sideways glances at church, at the grocery store and PTA meetings, the shoves in the locker room (*"What you looking at, faggot?"*), the insults that somehow fly right past me but I fear would peg each of them smack in the gut. They would quietly break friendships with everyone in town who spoke gay slurs, who were anti-gay, anti-Gooby. They might stop church altogether. They might feel the need to move. They would suffer it all and never breathe a complaint.

Because they love me.

"What you thinking about, Tretch?" Mom will ask me.

And I'll say, "Nothing, Mom."

Meanwhile, I feel like all my thoughts are shooting out from my eye sockets like slides on a projector screen: Matt haloed by the sun coming in through our English class window; Matt's dads dropping him off at school, and Matt introducing me; Matt reaching for my hand that day in church and keeping it there; Matt getting into the shower after gym class; Matt lying in my bed as I do homework at my desk, my heart feeling so full, sometimes so full I can't sleep at night, sometimes so full it aches, like I'm being stepped on.

She can see them all.

Or maybe she can't.

I mean, if it's not all that obvious to Matt, then maybe it's not all that obvious to anyone.

three

"So what are you doing right now?" A hot fog shoots from Matt's mouth as we cross the road to Barrow Street in our first hour of winter break.

"I don't know. What do you want to do?"

"Okay." He grabs my shoulders, looking me straight in the face, which makes it hard for me to not imagine kissing him. "Here's what I was thinking. One, we should go get hot chocolate and celebrate exams being over."

"You want to go to Mabel's?"

"Yes." Matt smiles. I know what the smile means, too. Amy Sinks works at Mabel's Drop-In & Dine, the best place to get hot chocolate in town. (Supposedly the secret is that they mix in Cool Whip and half-and-half with the cocoa powder.) She's only fifteen like us, but somehow she's been working there since September. Joe says they're probably paying her under the table. ("Sweet," Matt said when I informed him of this, like it made her some kind of undercover cop.)

I've always known Amy Sinks, and for as long as I've known her, she's been *beautiful*—and I mean that in the "drop dead" sense. She's got this long dark brown hair that's curly at its ends (naturally, too) and bright, December-birthstone eyes. I can remember the first time Matt saw her. It was only the second day of eighth grade, his second day in town, and we were sitting at a lunch table all by ourselves in the cafeteria when she walked by with a couple of her friends. She was laughing and shaking her head, making her curls bounce.

Matt nudged me and asked, "Who is *that* girl?" And I said, "That's Amy Sinks. Her dad owns the gymnastics place in town. Sinks's Young-'n-Fit."

Matt laughed. "What's it called?"

"Sinks's Young-'n-Fit," I repeated. I guess that's a pretty weird name for a gym for kids, but by that point it had never occurred to me to question it. Basically every kid in town goes to Sinks's Young-'n-Fit when they're little. If you're a girl, you usually take ballet lessons. If you're a boy, you do gymnastics.

"Pretty funny," Matt said. "But she *does* look fit." I turned and watched Amy Sinks swinging her hair.

"Yeah, I guess." Already I felt jealousy like a hot dry coal warming my stomach.

Nowadays, the coal's not really all that noticeable. I mean, it's there. I can still feel it. But now it's just kind of a dull lump, something I carry around.

"So what's the second thing?" I ask now. We're walking along Barrow Street. "You made it sound like you had two things."

"Oh! What are you doing tonight?"

I shrug. Truth: Even if I did have plans, I'd cancel them in a moment if he asked me to. "I don't know. You got a plan?"

"*King Kong* is showing at the Old Muse tonight." He leans toward me and claps his hands. "You *gotta* come. It's the 1976 version with Jeff Bridges. So cheesy, but so good."

I crack a smile. The Old Muse is an old theater in Samsanuk that Matt's dads moved down from New York to restore. Now they show all these ancient, artsy, and foreign movies there. I've actually never been, but Matt tells me about it all the time. He always ends up saying, "You gotta *come* sometime, man! Get your parents to bring you!" Samsanuk's a little bit of a drive, though, about thirty minutes away, which is far enough for Mom and Dad to conveniently tell me no every time I ask them to take me. Joe went once with his girlfriend, Melissa, and when he got home I asked him to tell me all about it. "It was really cool," he said. "I liked it a lot." But he didn't say anything about the movie, or whether he'd seen Matt's dads there.

"That sounds incredible," I say now to Matt. And it does. I can't think of anything I'd like to do more.

We talk about exams for a little bit. Matt is worrying about his geography grade. "Aw, come on," I say. "You know you did fine."

"Maybe not this time, though, Tretch." He sounds like he's really in doubt. "But no matter!" He spreads his arms out as he jumps over a frozen puddle. My heart leaps a little as he does. "Because it is *winter break at last!*" He spins around like Ebenezer Scrooge at the end of *A Christmas Carol*, then pounces off the curb into an empty parking space, beneath the sign that reads FOR EXPECTANT MOTHERS. Across from us, Warmouth's downtown scene is revving up, people going in and out of stores, emerging with bags and boxes, spending big money.

Mabel's Drop-In & Dine sits on the corner by the crosswalk. As we swing in and start rubbing our hands warm, Matt immediately scans the place for Amy Sinks. I remind myself that my version of what's happening is not the same as the real version of what's happening, and I need to switch over to the real version quick. *For your sake*, I remind myself. *This is for your sake, Tretch.*

Mabel's is practically empty, except for a few high schoolers I recognize but don't know, some nervous-looking ladies with shopping bags in their laps and scarves around their heads, and an old man—one of my granddad's friends. I look at him and nod as Matt and I seat ourselves at a booth. The old man tips the brim of his hat and winks. Matt catches me nodding and looks over his shoulder.

"I swear, Tretch, you know the most random people."

"What can I say? I'm just super popular." I shrug, as if to say *No big deal*, but Matt's too busy swiveling his head around every which way to notice. "You see her?" he asks, and right then Amy Sinks appears from the kitchen holding a tray with two cold sandwiches for the nervous ladies. She sees us immediately and opens her mouth in surprise.

"I wanted the barbecue chips," one of the nervous ladies complains.

"Oh, that's right," Amy says. "I'm so sorry." She flies back to the kitchen, winking at us—*both* of us—on the way, and in a split second returns with chips in hand. "Can I get you two anything else?" she asks. The ladies have their mouths full and shake their heads.

Next, she checks on the old man. "How you doing, Mr. Thumb?" she asks. I take note of his name. "Need anything?"

He nods and says loudly, "Tell that Farm boy to come talk to me a minute."

Matt gives a quiet chuckle and buries his head in his hands. "Why, Tretch," he singsongs, "you *are* popular."

Amy starts making her way to our booth. She always walks with a kind of dance in her step. One of the things that makes her so attractive, I guess. Matt swings his leg out and kicks me under our table.

"Tretch," Amy says when she gets to us. "I think your friend wants to see you."

"Ha," I say. "Okay." I stand up, and she slides into my side of the booth. Matt has a wild look of happiness on his face. "Hey, *hey*," he says. His hand goes to his forehead and brushes back some of the wavy thickness of his hair. He always lets it grow long in the winter.

I notice these things.

Like the way the temperature in Matt's face rises as Amy asks him what's going on. I crack a smile and turn. I know it's the right thing to do, to leave them alone for a little while. Since Matt likes her, and since he's my best friend, and since loving someone means wanting him to be happy even if it makes you sadder in the long run.

Mr. Thumb waves me into the seat across from him. I shake his hand before I sit down. "Hey, Mr. Thumb," I say, like I would've known his name if Amy hadn't said it first. "How are you?"

"Very well, Mr. Farm! How are you? I'm sorry, I don't remember your first name—"

"Tretch," I tell him. "That's a nickname, though. It's

kind of a distortion of Rich, which is short for Richard, which is my—"

"Your granddad's name."

"Yes, sir. You know this, of course."

"And your dad's name, too."

"Yes, sir, it is."

"And your mom's name is?"

"Katherine. Although she mostly goes by Katy."

He strokes some white tufts of hair growing from his chin. "Right, right. I think I remember. How's your old granddad doing?"

"Good." I look down at the empty space on the table in front of me. "He's, well, you know *him*."

"Ha-ha-ha! I sure do! Crazy old fart." Mr. Thumb chuckles for a moment. His plate is covered in sticky, hardened syrup. Flapjack residue. "Well, I don't know if you remember me, but I used to own that 501 Grocery down the way."

"Oh *yeah*," I say. Mr. Thumb used to give Granddad and me ice cream on the house. I remember now.

"I just wanted you to let your grandparents know how much my wife and I enjoyed our pickled okra last fall. I never get to see them to tell 'em myself." He grins and starts to pull at a scarf tied around his neck, a checkered design that alternates between deep blue and white. "My wife knitted this for your grandma not too long ago, and I've just been wearin' it around like it was meant for me." He pulls off the scarf and folds it into a square. "I was wondering if you would give it to its rightful owner."

"Well, of course I will," I say. I wonder if Mrs. Thumb knit the scarf for my grandmother because she was sick. I wonder if I should tell Mr. Thumb she's better now.

He slides the scarf across the table to me. "Thank you kindly, Mr. Farm."

I look at the blue-and-white square in my hands and feel its softness. "Your wife is *really* talented, Mr. Thumb."

The old man tips the brim of his hat like he did when I first made eye contact with him. "She certainly was," he says.

I look at the scarf again. I want to say something like *I'm sorry for your loss,* but I can't bring myself to say it for some reason. Maybe it just sounds too hollow inside my head.

So I just look up at Mr. Thumb and say the only thing I can think of, which is "Mr. Thumb, this will mean *a lot* to my grandma."

He nods, closing his eyes for a second, and I know he gets my meaning. "Thank you, Tretch." He smiles. "You take care now. And have a merry Christmas. Tell your family the same."

"I will," I say. I stand and shake his hand once more. "Merry Christmas, Mr. Thumb."

I walk back across the restaurant to the booth where Matt and Amy are seated, the scarf tucked safely under my arm. For a moment, they don't see me. He's laughing all nervous and hyena-like at a joke she just made, and she's wagging her head all exaggerated with her tongue lolling out. I hover for a moment before Matt registers I'm there.

"Here, Tretch, slide on in," he says, gesturing to the seat across from him. Like I'm not interrupting anything. Like I'm welcome here, belong here even. *Well, of course you belong here, Tretch, you big doof!* I can picture him saying it. Not a single ounce of me detects a single ounce of Matt wishing I wasn't there. In this restaurant. In this booth. I am stupidly thankful for it.

Amy slides out of the booth to make way for me, and I slide in, putting the scarf onto the place mat in front of me. I prop my elbow on the windowsill and look out. Clumps of Warmouthians bustle along in the cold outside.

"Was that, like, really weird?" Matt asks.

"Um . . ." I begin.

"*Ooh*, what's this?" Amy, still standing, reaches across the table for the scarf.

"His wife made it for my grandma," I explain. Then I whisper, "And then she died." Amy drops the scarf onto the table like I've just announced it was a leper baby's swaddling clothes.

"Yikes," she says.

I pick it up off the table, hoping Mr. Thumb hasn't seen. I am about to announce it's time for me to be leaving and maybe I'll see Matt later for the *King Kong* showing when the phone behind the cash register rings. "Hold on, boys," Amy says. She goes over to answer it, dancing her way to the counter. I start to wonder if the way she wags her butt while she does this is on purpose. *Is it possible that she likes Matt back?* I wonder. I look at Matt and he winks.

"So you never told me you were a dancer, Tretch," he says.

"*What?*"

"Amy told me. She said you guys have talked about dancing."

"*What?* No. I mean, I might have *mentioned* it to her, but we didn't *talk* about it."

"So we've been, like, best buds since I moved here, and you've never told me this." Matt has this smug look on his face. Teasing me, I know.

"Well, no offense or anything." I cough once. "But it's a little bit of a *secret*, you know? Let's face it—if word got out about my talent, I'd become famous overnight. I'd practically get whisked off to Broadway, and then who would you sit with during lunch?"

Matt nudges my forearm. "I'm just messing with you, Tretch. But seriously, what do you dance to?"

"Oh," I say. "Pop, mostly."

"What's your favorite?"

"To dance to?"

"Yeah."

" 'I Knew You Were Trouble.' Taylor Swift."

Matt slaps his forehead and laughs.

"*What?*" I can't even believe I'm having this conversation. I only ever mentioned dancing to Amy in the first place because her dad was looking for new songs to play during the Young-'n-Fit classes. Now I feel betrayed. "What else am I supposed to dance to, huh?"

A few more customers slip into Mabel's, and Amy gets busy serving them. When she has a moment, she slips us hot chocolate and French fries and slices of pie. It's all delicious, but Matt's so focused on her that he's forgetting to eat. Even when I crack a few jokes, he only ever responds with a "Hmpf," and I'm just like, *Are you serious right now?*

Then Amy comes over and lingers for a few seconds and he brightens right up, taking bites from his pie and saying, "God, this is good. Did you make this, Amy?" before she jets off to serve someone else. When she leaves, the conversation I have with him isn't really a conversation—it's just something to fill time between her visits.

After a while, we're just sitting there, wordlessly, with empty mugs and plates. Amy's on the phone, taking down another customer's order. When she's done, she pops back to our booth.

"I have a question," she says. "What are you two doing *right now?*"

Matt's about to have a hernia from his excitement. "Nothing!" he blurts. "We're doing nothing! Why? You want to come hang out?"

"That was an order from the Jim Cho's Santa Claus. He wants a roast beef and pastrami sandwich, but he needs it delivered. Can you guys, by any chance, run it over to him? You can keep the tip if he gives you one."

I can feel Matt's disappointment. He's not ready to leave her. "Sure thing," he says, but the words drag. Amy's oblivious.

"Okay, *great*," she says. "I'll go whip it up really fast." She disappears again.

Matt looks at me and sighs. "I thought she was about to ask us to do something."

"I know," I say, "but, hey, it's not like she asked us *not* to do something."

Matt shrugs, and I give a trying smile, aka the smile that says, *I'm trying to make you happy, even though it's so clearly not going to work*. There's a copy of *The Mouth*, Warmouth's local newspaper, sitting on the table next to ours. I snag it.

"Wow," I say. "Look at that." I push the paper over to Matt. The headline reads:

STARS FALL ON WARMOUTH!
METEOR SHOWER FRIDAY NIGHT AT 10

"Oh, nice," he says.

"We'll have to remember to watch for it later."

"Yeah." Matt stares into his hot chocolate. "So, I'm sorry we have to go to Jim Cho's now. I know you hate that place."

I swipe my hand through the air. "Nah, I just hate the smell of it."

"It sucks that she's the only person working. I mean, if she wasn't, she could come with. Aren't there, like, child labor laws protecting her against this kind of thing?"

I tilt my empty mug and stare into it. "I don't know, Matt. Why don't you hang around until Mabel gets in and ask her?"

"Maybe I will."

"Oh, I was joking . . ."

"No, I mean, maybe I'll stay," he clarifies. "Not to ask about child labor laws. If that's cool. Maybe I'll just hang around and see when she gets off."

I get it then. I realize he's asking *me* to take on the Jim Cho's Santa Claus delivery responsibility.

"Oh, uh," I say, "okay. I, uh—" *It's fine, Tretch*, I tell myself. *It's on your way home anyway.* "I'll just run by Jim Cho's, uh, by myself . . ."

"Man, *thanks*, Tretch."

Matt Gooby is many things. Considerate 100 percent of the time is not one of them.

I could be pretty ticked off, I guess. But I'm not really. I'll get to run by the bookstore, which happens to be located right next to Jim Cho's. (It's the bookstore with the most notoriously stupid name in the world—and, no, it's not called We

Got Books! or Books Galore, or anything even remotely catchy like either of those semi-lame names. No, the name of the Warmouth bookstore is simply Books. Just plain old Books. How dumb is that?)

"No problem, amigo. I wanted to go by Books, anyway," I tell him. "I need a book for break."

Matt has nothing to say to that. He's not a big reader.

I wonder what will happen if he and Amy keep hitting it off. I wonder if my invitation to *King Kong* has disappeared.

Well, maybe that's for the better, I think. After all, Mom and Dad are going to say no anyways. And I always hate making excuses for them. It's one thing to say *Mom and Dad don't want to drive me the thirty miles to Samsanuk and waste the gas.* It's even more of a thing to say *Mom and Dad don't want me to go because they're uncomfortable with the idea of me being seen with a family that has two dads.* I think there's always this fear for them that Matt and I might be seen as Warmouth's new (and second ever, I guess) gay couple, despite the number of times I assure them that Matt is *not* gay.

After the note today, a night on the town with Matt and his dads would probably be as good as a double date as far as Warmouth gossip standards are concerned.

I can hear it now, like a disembodied voice from a faraway telephone: *"I heard Richard and Katy's boy is going steady with that Gooby boy now."* My mom and dad would crush the rumors: *"They're just* friends! *Tretch has always flocked to the underdogs!"* and unknowingly add to the already mega-thick layer of camouflage around me.

I whistle the tune to "Jingle Bell Rock," partly because it's in my head, partly to remind Matt that he isn't talking. It doesn't register with him; his eyes are on the kitchen door.

"You know," I say, "it hasn't really, like, *hit* me that it's finally winter break." A weak last-ditch attempt at conversation.

"Yeah, me neither," Matt replies. "To be honest, I'm pretty ready to ship off to old NYC."

"You'll have to give me a call," I say. "And let me know what shows you and your dads go see."

"I think they already bought tickets for *Hedwig.*"

"Oh, well, that will be cool."

"You think she thinks I'm gay, Tretch?"

"Hm?"

"Amy." Matt looks me dead-on, and I know he wants an honest answer.

I blink a couple times. "Well," I say, "I mean, she might think that . . . I mean, you don't *act* like it or anything, but—" In my mind, I am slapping my own forehead.

"You think she thinks *we're* gay? Like, *together*?"

I just stare across the booth, noticing a clock on the wall that has Mickey Mouse ears and tiny little gloved hands.

After a moment, I shrug, a dry lump sitting in my throat.

"I mean, surely not," I say. "There's no way."

"Yeah, you're right. I don't know why I was even worried." Matt slumps down into the cushion of his seat and crosses his arms. I picture him with a cigarette hanging out of his mouth, in a black-and-white photo. I think it would be hard for Matt to not look good under any circumstance, even with his brown hair getting bushier in the wintertime, even when he's sulking. But the way I'm picturing him right now, he looks *really* good.

"Sometimes I just want a *sign*, Tretch," he says. "To, like, wear around my neck or something, that says, *I'm not gay!*"

Boy, I bet your dads would be proud to hear that, I think. But I guess I understand.

Sometimes I want a sign that says just the opposite.

four

Amy reappears with a white Styrofoam to-go box and a big smile on her face. She moves to hand the to-go box to Matt, but I intercept it.

"I'll be the delivery boy," I explain. "It's on my way."

"You're a lifesaver, Tretch," she says, sliding a ponytail holder off of her wrist and gathering her hair behind her neck. "Mabel just got on to me for not wearing my hair up." She rolls her eyes. "Whatever."

Matt laughs hard at that, taking a bunch of short little breaths and slapping himself in the chest. He has a pretty hard chest.

I watch Amy smiling. Her eyelashes flap. I wonder if she's noticing.

"Well, see ya," I say, scrambling out, not giving them a chance to say good-bye, just in case both of them are too distracted with each other to realize I'm going.

That doesn't stop me from looking back, though. Once I'm outside, I see Amy writing something down on a napkin for Matt. He stares with his mouth open. She hands the napkin over to him before heading back to the kitchen.

Matt turns to look at me, like he knew I'd be there. He waves the napkin around ecstatically. I don't even have to look closely to know there's a phone number on it.

I can't help but be happy for him. Honest. I'm not even faking when I say that. I mean, sure, I probably know somewhere in my brain that I'll be sad about it later, but who would rather feel that, right?

No, in that moment, watching Matt's face blush a nice shade of red, feeling probably better than he's felt all year—that's something that can only make me feel good. I'm not even mad about having to take the sandwich to Jim Cho's by myself.

Through the air, I give Matt a high five.

He presses his hand against the glass, a high five back.

I rush into Jim Cho's to do my delivery. It's really nothing against the place, but I can't stand the smell of it. I think it has to do with this time when my family ate Chinese food before flying out to Dallas to see Nana and Papa one Easter. I got super nervous on the plane right before takeoff and I threw up a little bit in my barf bag. Lucky for me no one noticed, but I clenched that barf bag close to me the whole flight just in case it happened again, and the whole time I could smell it—*airport Chinese food barf.*

I deliver the food without incident, and, no, I don't get a tip. Then I plunge back out into the fresh-ish winter air outside. There's just the smell of the cold downtown, kind of a sweet smell, like a sugar cookie.

This year's Warmouth Holiday Tree, a big, tall, dark, bushy-looking thing, stands on the front lawn of the courthouse. The tree-lighting ceremony isn't for another couple nights. This year, I have to sing in the choir, since Mom made me join after she heard me singing "Ave Maria" in the shower.

The courthouse is huge and square, and outside of it is a statue of a Confederate soldier from Warmouth. The plaque beneath it reads: *William Griggers. The brave shall know nothing of death.* He holds a sword in one hand and a hat in the other. He is smiling.

I think sometimes about how fake that is.

Surely William Griggers, when he was alive, didn't smile like this, or carry his sword and hat around casually at the same time. Not after the war, anyway, I wouldn't guess. Joe says most soldiers come back from war torn up with broken hearts. "You remember Uncle Dennis?" Joe asked when he was explaining this to me. "Yeah," I said, but it was a stretch. Uncle Dennis (my dad's uncle, so technically my great-uncle) hanged himself a long time ago—in our grandparents' backyard, actually. It was a couple years after he came back from Vietnam, and he was experiencing severe post-traumatic stress disorder, and "probably," Joe explained to me, "some other things, too."

When I asked him what he meant, Joe said, "Basically, something happened to him in the war that messed him up pretty bad, something so bad he couldn't shake it, not even after he got home." When I asked Dad about it, he said it was weird; basically, Uncle Dennis could be normal half the time and completely off his rocker the rest of the time. Dad said once he walked in on Uncle Dennis standing on top of the sofa and peeing onto the Farm family TV set. I laughed at that, but Dad said it wasn't funny. Actually, he said, it was a little scary.

I think, before he died, Grandma and Granddad tried to get Uncle Dennis to move into a home where he could get proper care. When Uncle Dennis found out about this, though, he said he wouldn't go, and to prove his point, he . . . well, you know.

"Did you see it, Dad?" I asked. "Did you see him after—?"

"No." My dad shook his head. "But your granddad did. Saw his own brother all dead and hanging like that." I started to feel queasy. A little while after, Joe walked into my room.

"*Tretch*," he said. "What's *up*, dude?"

"Joe, I'm so glad you're alive," I said, and he stood there for a moment, looking at me. I remember he was wearing boxers, an undershirt, and a pair of knee socks. He had on his glasses. He came over to me, bent down, and hugged me.

"I love you, Tretch," he said. I think that's the only time one of us has ever said that to the other.

It's a strange thing to be thinking about as I push the door open to Books and trigger the little bell near the ceiling. I try to wipe all emotion from my face and keep my eyes on the floor.

Please, God, I pray, *let it be Lana Kramer's day off.*

Lana Kramer is in ninth grade, too. She wears big glasses and turtleneck sweaters and heavy eye makeup. Joe once called her a "hipster kid," which made me ask him, "Joe, aren't you a hipster?" to which he answered, "Well, maybe." He *does* have big glasses, and he likes old things—books, movies, clothes, stuff like that. But all that stuff makes Joe *interesting*. And for some reason it just makes Lana Kramer a know-it-all. Like when I told her I didn't like *The Great Gatsby*, and she said, "Well, you might be too young to actually *get it*."

I was so mad that day I had to walk out of Books empty-handed—which was especially unfortunate because Mom was there, and she was all, "Tretch, pick out something you want. My treat."—because, as a matter of fact, I *did* "get" *The Great Gatsby*. And I would even go so far as to say I got it *better* than Lana Kramer. I mean, *I* picked up on Nick Carraway being gay and actually had to *tell* that to Lana Kramer.

"What?" she had said. "No, he's *not*."

"He is."

"He's totally *not*."

"He is."

Then I showed her the passage that says it all, on page thirty-eight of my paperback edition, right smack at the end of chapter two.

"You could read that *a lot* of ways, Tretch!" she contested after she read it. But I don't think so. I mean, for the whole book Nick Carraway is totally *obsessed* with Jay Gatsby. I mean, that's why the story he's narrating is called *The Great Gatsby* and not something like *Daisy Is Crazy*.

I'm probably narrating a book right now called *The Great Gooby* and don't even realize it.

I try to put thoughts of Matt out of my mind and shrug over to the paperback new release section, where I'll be safe to sneak a peek at the front desk. Sure enough, when I look up, I see Lana Kramer there in the flesh, wearing a pink cardigan and stamping the inside covers of used books, prepping them for resale.

"Hey, Tretch," she says, seeing me through the shelves with her new pair of pink-framed glasses. "Back for more Fitzgerald? Or will we be reading, yawn, Salinger today?"

It's creepy how you remember all the books I buy, I think.

"Uh," I say. "Really just looking today."

"Well, I'm obligated to tell you, there's a sale this week on all young adult fantasy paperbacks." She closes the book she was stamping and moves it onto a stack. "That covers your Twilight, your Hunger Games, and your Harry Potter." She clears her throat. "Not that *you* would be interested in any of those, Mr. Literature."

That embarrasses me. "Thanks, Lana," I say. "I actually like Twilight. Problem is, I've already read them all."

"Team Edward or Team Jacob?" Lana asks me, one eyebrow arched.

"Jacob," I say. "I like pulling for the underdog. Plus, it totally sucks getting friend-zoned."

"Sucks getting placed second banana to a vampire who sparkles in the sunlight." Lana smiles. "Still, he's smoking hot in the movies—"

"Smo-kin'," I agree.

Lana squinches her eyebrows.

"Sarcasm," I blurt. "Yeah, poor Jacob. Dumped by Bella in the books, dumped by Taylor Swift in real life."

"Psh, whatever. I bet he was *glad* to be rid of her. She's so dramatic and all—"

"You don't like Taylor Swift?" I ask. "I love Taylor Swift."

"Ugh." Lana Kramer scrunches her face and sings in a mock whiny voice while shaking her shoulders. " '*I knew you were trouble when you walked iiiiin.*' Can't stand her."

I need to find a book and get out fast.

"You ever read *A Separate Peace*?" she asks me.

"Nope."

Lana is holding a paperback in her hand. "Here," she says. She gives it a few pumps and sails it over rows of historical fiction and nonfiction. I catch it safely. "Oh," I say. On the cover there's a young guy sitting at a window with his knees up around his chin. He looks cold and sad and lonely.

"This looks—" I start.

"Amazing?" Lana finishes for me. Her eyes are big behind her glasses. I check out the price tag on the cover. Six bucks.

"Just take it," she says. "On the house."

"Oh. Are you sure? You won't get in trouble—"

She swats her hand in the air. *"Please.* My boss is my cousin. What's he gonna do?"

"Thanks, Lana." I feel bad just taking the freebie and not buying anything, though. "I'll, uh . . . I'll look around some more, too, if you don't mind."

"Oh." She looks down. "Sure thing, Tretch. No problem. I, uh, I won't distract you so much this time." She gives a quick smile without looking me in the face, and I wander the shelves a little while longer.

I'm in the classics section, which feels right. I want something BIG. Something that will be a challenge for my two weeks off.

There are three F. Scott Fitzgerald books: *Tender Is the Night*, *This Side of Paradise*, *Gatsby*. There's some Hemingway: *The Snows of Kilimanjaro and Other Stories*, *The Old Man and the Sea*, *The Sun Also Rises*, *A Farewell to Arms*. Of course there are Jane Austen and Charles Dickens. I haven't read either of them since the abridged copies of *Pride and Prejudice* and *Oliver Twist* I got in the second grade. I hold a copy of *Pride and Prejudice* in my hand, then set it back on the shelf and trade it for a copy of *Finnegans Wake*. I weigh it in my hand, maybe the thickest book I've ever held, not counting the Bible. I put it back on the shelf and keep looking.

Moby Dick, *Wuthering Heights*, *Silas Marner*, *Little Women*, *Their Eyes Were Watching God*. I linger on *Their Eyes Were Watching God* for a minute, but finally I stick it back. *Not quite it*, I think. A book with a tattered, faded blue spine catches my eye and I free it from the shelf. It's *On the Road* by Jack Kerouac, and on its cover is a black-and-white picture, like the one I pictured Matt sitting in, of two men standing close together. They are both facing the camera with sly half smiles and their hands in their pockets. One of them has his head cocked to the side.

I feel Lana Kramer's stare.

"What you got there?" she asks.

"*On the Road*, Jack Kerouac." I mispronounce the last name, which makes Lana laugh.

"It's pronounced like 'Karrow-ack,' not 'Kirrow-ock.'"

"Ah," I say, and it bothers me that I've given her the chance to show off.

"Might go over your head. Then again, I told you the same thing about *Gatsby*."

I look at Lana Kramer stamping books for a minute. I notice how she isn't quite making eye contact. And then I realize something that makes me happy and sad at the same time.

Lana Kramer has a crush on me.

The best thing that could happen would be if I fell in love with Lana Kramer. But that could never happen because really, like, it's actually impossible.

I take the Karrow-ack book to the counter. "I think this is the one," I say.

Lana rings it up for me on the cash register. "Okay. Six dollars and one cent." I pull a five and a one from my blue Velcro wallet, which makes an embarrassing ripping sound as I open it. The change part is, I find, empty.

Lana sees me searching and says, "Oh, no worries about the penny, Tretch."

"Wow," I tell her. "Two deals today."

"Well, it *is* the holiday season." Lana manages a smile at this. Her glasses slide down to the point of her nose. "Take it easy, Tretch. Enjoy those." She points to the books now placed in the crook of my arm. *A Separate Peace* by John Knowles, *On the Road* by Jack Kerouac. I think it's funny and kind of cool that the authors share the same initials. That kind of stuff always makes me feel like things are meant to be. Maybe they'll teach me something I don't already know about love, about being in love, or even just about being a person.

"Take it easy, Lana," I say, careful to make sure it doesn't sound anything more than friendly.

Once I'm outside the shop, I linger for a minute to spy through the shopwindow. I see Lana putting a wad of singles from her own pocket into the cash register. She's paying for the copy of *A Separate Peace*. Then I see her digging even deeper into her pockets.

A penny emerges from her left hand, and she places it into the cash drawer.

five

When I get home, I knock on Joe's bedroom door, though of course he's not in there—he's with his girlfriend, Melissa. I edge the door open ever so slightly and notice that his decorative lights, little red bulbs encased in these little Chinese takeout boxes, are still on, and I wonder if they've been on all day. After I unplug the cord from the wall, I do what I always do when I find myself alone in Joe's room: I look around.

Joe's walls are my favorite walls.

For starters, there are all these record sleeves tacked to them. College radio bands like Youth Lagoon, The Drums,

Washed Out, and Zola Jesus, just to name a few. Oh, and
Sufjan Stevens. I like to listen to Sufjan Stevens when the
house is empty and I don't feel like practicing my dance
moves. He sings a lot about being in love in all of these different scenarios, which I like. And better yet, he puts them into
stories.

Like, for example, there's this one song he sings about a
boy (I'm *pretty* sure it's a boy) who's got cancer, and it's sung
from the perspective of his best friend. At one point in the
song, the best friend kisses the boy who's got cancer, and there
are all of these great scenes where they're almost touching and
stuff, and then there is this one line about the father finding
out about them. It's really beautiful—and sad, too, because of
course the boy with cancer dies in the end, leaving the best
friend to try to make sense of it all.

When I talked to Joe about the song, he said I impressed
him, like he didn't think I really listened to lyrics and thought
about them as much as I did. I asked Joe if he thought Sufjan
was gay because of my theory about the song being about two
boys, and Joe just tipped his head to the side. "Hmm, I don't
know," he said, and I nodded. I was about to cover my tracks—
say "Just a thought" or something like that—but Joe added,
"Although I don't really see how that makes much of a differ-
ence. I mean, it's not like I would like him any less."

I couldn't help but wonder what he meant by it. Like, was
he trying to tell me something?

The phone rings. I run downstairs to the kitchen to answer it. I get there in four rings and snatch the phone from its cradle.

"Hel-*lo*?" My voice comes in an unintentional blast.

"Tretch?"

Oh my God.

"*Matt?*"

"Tretch."

"Matt!"

He chuckles. "You sound excited to hear from me."

"I am!"

Okay, Tretch, dial it back a few notches, why don't you?

"Did you get the all-systems-go from your parents about *Kong* tonight?"

"Uh, no." I run the phone—thank God I chose the wireless—up the stairs to my room. "I, um, well, I kind of suspected it was off since . . ."

"Well, *that's* the thing. Amy's saying she can go now, so I'm having a total freak-out moment. I—I need you to be there. I mean, holy Jesus, what are we even supposed to talk about?"

"You just be yourself, Matt," I advise.

"Just tell your parents you're doing me a favor, Tretch, because I'm a hopeless case with girls, and I *need* you. Tell them I need you like no other, Tretch."

Mom and Dad, I'll say. *Matt needs me.*

"Okay," I tell him.

"Do not take no for an answer."

I know, I know.

"Are your parents driving?" I ask. "Do I even have technical permission from them?"

"Yes, Pop is driving. Dad is doing some introduction before the movie starts so he's going separately. And you have their full and *unconditional* permission."

"Awesome," I say. "I'll let you know."

"Call back."

"I will. Bye."

"Bye."

I have to make this happen.

Mom is wrapping presents in her room. I can hear through the closed door the unspooling of wrapping paper from its cardboard middle and the rusty *shing* of the scissors. I knock.

"Mom?"

"Yes, Tretch?" Her voice is mildly panicked. "Uh, hold on just a minute . . ."

"Got it," I assure her, putting my hands in my pockets. When she opens the door, I take them out.

"Thanks for knocking," she says, smiling. "It speaks to your personal integrity."

"Ha! Why, thank you, Mother," I say—and it's apparently a little too much because she looks at me with squinty eyes, suspicious.

"So who was that on the phone, hm?" she asks. "Lana Kramer?"

Mom overheard my conversation with Lana about *Gatsby*. I guess she felt the tension and misinterpreted it.

"Uh, no," I say. "It was Matt."

"Oh yeah? What's he up to?"

"Well, he's asked me to go to the movies with him and with . . . with Amy Sinks. You know, Young-'n-Fit."

"I know who Amy Sinks is." She smiles again. "Beautiful girl."

I nod once, so basically I'm just hanging my head. "Yeah, well, she and Matt are going to the movies and . . ."

"Tretch, I'm not going to let you go and encroach on that poor boy's date. He needs his space."

I snap my neck up then, so drastically it pops. "Mom, *what*? Are you kidding me? You never let me ride out to the Old Muse."

"Come on now. You two are together all the time. When you have a car and can drive yourself to the Old Muse, that'll be fine."

"But, Mom, please. Mr. Landon is driving."

"Tretch, *enough*. I'm sorry, but you boys are going to have to learn not to depend on each other quite so much. If Matt is taking a girl out to the movies, then you need to let him do just that. Let *him* take *her*. Without you."

"But—"

"And *you* do the good friend thing to do, which is call him right now and tell him you'll be waiting up for a phone call from him later. He can tell you all about it then."

"But, Mom, it's not that."

"Well, then, what is it?"

I swallow. What I say next comes up in a blurt like it's been pocketed away for a while. "But Lana! They've invited Lana!"

It is a bald-faced lie, which is honestly not something I'm super accustomed to telling. Especially with Mom. God, I feel so bad. Especially now that said bald-faced lie is making her face light up all huge. "*Really?*" she asks. "Oh, Tretch, that—"

And the bald-faced lie works.

"—that changes *everything*, sweetie. Why didn't you tell me that to begin with, huh?"

"Uh. I don't know." I shrug. "I guess it just made me feel embarrassed or something. I don't know." Mom opens her arms and I move right into them—and I'm not sure why exactly, maybe the guilt from lying or something, but I suddenly feel like I'm about to cry.

She mashes her cheek against my forehead. "A double date." Her breath flutters against my ear. "So you probably need some money, huh?"

I know at this point I don't even have to say it. But I'm generally a pretty straitlaced guy.

"No, I don't need money," I croak.

"Any thoughts on what you're going to wear?"

"Uh, not sure." I pull back from our hug, spinning away so she won't see my face. She can always tell. "I'll go survey my options and let you know."

I flee.

Upstairs in my room, my options are:

A) a white T-shirt with Edward Scissorhands on the front

B) Joe's old, handed-down black *Rubber Soul* tee

C) jeans, inevitably

D) my brown loafers with the tassel laces Matt likes

E) my regular old red Converse

F) nothing because I'm calling the whole night off on account of how guilty I feel about lying to Mom

G) come clean to Mom, say I'm sorry, and when she asks why I lied, just say, "I don't know. I don't even really understand it myself." That would be the truth, sort of.

I pull on a fresh pair of jeans, a darker pair that I like, and unfold the *Rubber Soul* shirt from my drawer. Joe doesn't miss the shirt much anymore since he's outgrown it, but it used to be his favorite. After I slide out of the polo I wore to school and slip into the tee myself, I start to think it might be my favorite shirt, too. It looks great on me—not too baggy, which is a hard find for someone who's a string bean like me.

In the bathroom, I say "Okay" to my reflection, pull a comb from the drawer beneath the sink, and rake it over my scalp a few times before replacing it. I look good—not great or anything, but good. Good enough to decide that it would be a waste if I didn't go. I dig my hands into the crumpled heap of sheets on my bed and pull out the cordless phone.

The phone rings only once before he answers, like he's been waiting.

"*Hello?*" His voice is loud, and I swear there's a smile in it.

"Hey."

"So we'll pick you up in an hour?"

I smile back.

"We'll be picking Lana up later," I explain to Mom, just in case she happens to glimpse the inside of the car and see my lack of a date. "Like, after Mr. Gooby picks me up."

"Sounds good." Mom doesn't ask me which Mr. Gooby it will be. Instead, she licks her thumb and, before I have time to protest, wipes it against my lip.

"Mom—" I jerk my head back.

"Well, I'm sorry, Tretch-o, but it looks like you've got a smudge of toothpaste or something."

"I'll get it," I say, and scratch furiously at the corner of my mouth.

"Are you nervous?"

"Mom, no. Geez." But the thing is—I am. I look out the window. "I hope Dad's home soon," I say, though I'm seriously totally hoping he doesn't get back from work until Matt's swooped in and successfully vamoosed with me in tow.

"I think he's stopping in at Jim Cho's to grab some take-out," Mom says. "He called a few minutes ago."

Perfect, I think. *Now come on, Goobys, come on.* At that exact moment, like I'm magic or something, they round the corner onto Watercress Road. I'm feeling crazy enough that I do this little half-jump/half-shriek thing that makes Mom tip her head to the side in a nurturing but *get your act together* kind of way. My hand is on the doorknob. "Okay, I'm out," I say. "They're here. That's them. I love you, Mom."

"Love you, too, Tretch-o." And then, I swear to God, she's crying. Not in a suddenly-sobbing kind of way, but her eyes are definitely filling up.

"Mom!" I take a step forward. Then, sure enough, oh my God it's my eyes, too. Everything goes all misty. "Mom, you can't start crying because you know it always makes *me* start."

"Oh, Tretch," she says. "Get out of here. Go on before you get messy." She flaps her hand at me like a bird's wing. "Go, go."

I spin around and pull the door open—"Okay-bye-I-love-you-bye-I'm-going-now"—and step out onto the porch, pulling the door closed.

The Goobys' red Volvo makes its way down Watercress. For all of five seconds, as the Volvo slows to a halt, I practice breathing exercises. I don't stop until Matt pushes the door open.

"Yo," he says.

"Yolo," I respond, and he gives me that *you're such a goof* look. I smile, and he smiles, and I don't realize that I'm totally lost in it until he says, "Tretch, I love this driveway as much as you do, but we got places to be."

"What?" I try to look shocked. "You mean you don't want to hang out by the mailbox all night long?" I slide into the backseat beside him. "What could be better than that?"

Landon is laughing in the driver's seat. "Hey, Tretch," he says, twisting in his seat, beard dragging across his shoulder. "How ya been, bud?"

"I'm good, Mr. Landon. Never better, in fact. Love the beard."

"Glad to hear it, and thanks!" He puts the car in reverse to back out of the driveway. Matt purses his lips and inflates the space beneath his nose with breath. Then he lets it go. "I'm nervous as all get-out," he whispers.

I nod. "It's gonna be great."

"By 'it,' do you mean the movie, the meteor shower, or the romantic conquest?"

"Can I opt for all of the above?"

Matt nods, and I realize maybe I should have said "*You're going to be great*" instead. Maybe it's not too late. Maybe I could say it now. I could say he looks handsome, which he does, and I could list off every charm he possesses. I could assure him that everything he says is witty and smart in its own way, that the way he views everything through a set of glass-half-full eyes makes him kind of heroic. I could say he's a great storyteller. I could say that maybe sometimes he could be a better listener, pay closer attention to things, be more sensitive. But I don't say a word. We sit in nervous silence on the way to Amy's house.

So much for my giving great advice.

Of course, when Amy Sinks appears, she looks amazing.

"Wow-ee," Matt says. "Just look at her."

Landon turns around in the driver's seat.

I'm looking at her as she struts over.

"Well, does one of you boys want to sit up front? Chauffeuring two people around is bad enough, but chauffeuring *three*—that's just demeaning."

That's my cue. I don't even have to wait for Matt to look at me with his pleading eyes. "Oh, yeah," I say. "I'll hop up there with you, Mr. Landon."

"Thanks, Tretch-o," he says. It's funny how everyone seems to think that's a good nickname for me. Like I need a nickname for my name, which is already a nickname, which is already a nickname.

I respond, "No problem-o," which I think is pretty clever. "Now, you guys will get some"—I cup my hand around Matt's knee; is that suspicious?—"quality time together pre-movie."

It's pretty wild to be a witness to your best friend's first date. And I can't help but think about what Mom said back at the house: *You boys are going to have to learn not to depend on each other quite so much.*

I wonder if Landon thinks the same thing, if he gave Matt a similar lecture. I can't quite picture it—but I guess there's gotta be at least two sides to every parent.

"I don't know how *quality* it'll be in the backseat of your pop's Volvo," Landon says, flashing a glance at Matt in the rearview.

When I step out, I hold the car door open for Amy. Her hair is still in the Mabel's ponytail. But she's got on a new pair of jeans and—this slays me—a *Rubber Soul* T-shirt. Like, how many teenagers in Warmouth have *Rubber Soul* T-shirts? Granted, hers is kind of feminized, but it's still, like . . . awkward.

She's also slurping off the last bits of a Popsicle. Like, first off, who eats a Popsicle in the middle of winter? And, second, who doesn't bring enough for the whole party? And, *third*, INNUENDO MUCH?

"Hey-o, Tretch-o," she says. Her lips are red and shimmery. "Nice shirt."

"Yeah," I say.

She giggles. "We're like the same person."

"I know, right? Tasty Popsicle?"

"Tasty Popsicle. Here, you can have my joke." She hands me the Popsicle stick. I read it as I walk around to the front seat, trying to ignore Matt's cheesy "Hey, Amy, you look nice," and her "I like to think I clean up *fairly* well."

The joke on the Popsicle stick is this: What do you find in the middle of NOWHERE?

I turn the stick over in my hand for the answer.

The letter "H."

Ha.

I slide into the passenger seat next to Landon, who is introducing himself to Amy. They shake hands. "It's nice to meet you," she says, and it's the first time I've seen her act even a little shy. There's kind of a weird silence as we pull out of her driveway, so I ask, "Y'all want to hear a joke? What do you find in the middle of NOWHERE?"

I watch Landon as he considers.

"How about an art house theater?" Matt suggests, and Landon reaches back and pops him in the knee.

"Hey!" Landon says. "I take offense."

That cuts the tension pretty well because everyone starts laughing. Then the conversation starts to flow. Nobody even cares to hear the answer to the joke.

Matt's *other* dad, the one he actually calls *Dad*, is already at the Old Muse, preparing his introduction. When Amy finds out we're not seeing the original 1933 *King Kong* but its 1976 remake, starring Jessica Lange, she's super excited.

"Oh my God, I love her," she proclaims as we stand in front of the movie poster outside the Old Muse. It's the original poster design, too, with the appropriate tagline—*For Christmas*—in red letters at the bottom.

"This version of *King Kong* was released on December 17, 1976," Landon explains. "So we try and show it every year around Christmastime to pay tribute. It was a pretty big movie for Ron and me."

"Was it your first date?" I ask, and immediately I'm embarrassed.

Because of course it wasn't. Matt's dads aren't that old.

Landon smiles. "Well, I was twelve and Ron was nine, so neither one of us was quite there yet. But it scared the bejesus out of both of us when we were kids. And we did see it again together in college."

"On a date?" Amy presses, and I'm kind of glad she does because I want to know more.

Landon nods. "Yes, on a date. Well . . . shall we entrée?"

Landon pulls the door to the Old Muse open, and I feel like my world is about to open up. When I step through the door I realize it's a world of dimly lit, popcorn-smelling, conversation-buzzing, alcoholic-beverage-serving excitement. The line to the bar/box office is extreeeemely long, so apparently this whole annual *King Kong* showing is a big deal.

But, *Jesucristo*, the inside of this place—it's amazing. The front hallway from the entrance is designed like an alleyway, with red brick walls and stuff, and there are these really awesome life-size, cardboard cutouts of famous movie characters stationed along the way, as if they're all saying, "Welcome to the Old Muse!"

"Welcome to the Old Muse!" says Samuel L. Jackson from *Pulp Fiction*. "Welcome to the Old Muse," says Cher from *Moonstruck*. "Welcome to the Old Muse!" say Audrey Hepburn and Sidney Poitier and Anne Bancroft and . . .

"Jessica Lange!"

Amy weaves her hand inside the cardboard elbow and stands like she's expecting someone to take a picture. I think it's annoying until I spot one of Jimmy Stewart and go kind of nutso myself. It's from the scene in *It's a Wonderful Life* when Jimmy Stewart, as the mega-down-on-his-luck George Bailey, is walking on the bridge all drunk and desperate. I can tell it's from that scene because his lip is cut from the bar fight and there's snow in his hair.

It's a Wonderful Life is probably my favorite movie of all time.

Landon takes out his iPhone and says, "Here, all of you pose." So we gather around George Bailey. "Merry Christmas, Mr. Potter," I say in my best Jimmy Stewart voice (which is not as good as Joe's Jimmy Stewart voice, but, oh well) as Landon snaps the picture.

"Should we wait in line, Pop?" Matt asks, but Landon shakes his head. "Nah, we're VIPs tonight. Let's go in and get seats."

Immediately, we file through the theater door. I follow Matt down the aisle, not realizing what I'm doing until I get to our row of seats. "Oh, pardon me," I say, stepping back to let Amy cross in front of me. Of course she and Matt will want to be next to each other. But she smiles, shaking her head, and says, "Oh no, Tretch, after you."

I stand my ground, firmly but also unsure. "Uhh . . . okay." As I move down the row toward the seat next to Matt, I can't help but think, *Oh God, oh God, what have I done?*

Because, of course, now I'm sitting *between* them.

I do a sideways glance at Matt to see if he's angry or not, and I honestly can't tell at first because he's all leaned forward in silence, staring at the blank movie screen. Seconds pass, I think a whole minute passes, and I can't even say anything because there's this weird static in my head. On the one hand, I might have messed things up—but it wasn't really my fault, was it? After all, Amy had said, "After you." And, on the other hand, hey—

I *am* sitting next to Matt. And I will be for the next, uh . . . "Hey, how long is this movie?" I ask. Matt turns his head. He's smiling all big. He's not a bit upset.

"Oh, like, two hours, I think," he says. "Not too long. Why, you gotta pee?"

I shake my head. "Oh, no. Just curious."

For the next *two hours*, I get to sit next to Matt in a dark room.

From down the aisle, there's a smooching sound and I turn. It's a reflex, I guess, to turn when you hear smooching. I see Ron is bent over Landon's upturned face. It's a quick smooch, but Matt goes, "Oh my gosh" and rolls his eyes. "Hi, Dad," he says. "Dad, meet Amy."

Immediately, Ron does this funny thing where he reaches to me for a handshake and says, "Nice to meet you, Amy."

I laugh, but Matt is not amused. *"Dad—"*

"Kidding, kidding. Nice to meet you, Amy." Ron smiles at her, and she laughs and accepts his hand. "Nice to meet you, too, Mr. Ron." They shake, and Ron winks at me. "You'll have to excuse my joke, Tretch. I'm extremely nervous about giving this speech to a full house."

Right then, the lights start to dim in the theater.

Ron flashes a nervous glance at us. "That's my cue." He jets down the aisle to the little platform in front of the screen.

"Hi, folks," he says once he gets there, and immediately every-one in the audience begins to clap. Ron goes beet red. "Without further ado, I want to thank you all for coming to our special annual, wintry showing of *King Kong*, a movie that's meant a lot to me ever since I was a kid who saw it—too young, I might add—in theaters, and which came to mean a lot *more* to me as an adult, when I was able to see it on a big screen—in an art house just like this one—with the man who would eventually become my husband."

A ripple of "aw" sounds spreads throughout the audience. Landon smiles. Meanwhile, Ron is a brighter red than ever. "Did I say 'without further ado'?" he asks, and everyone cheers. He hops off the stage, flies up the aisle, and pulls down the seat next to Landon's.

Landon whispers something to Ron, and Ron smiles. I look at Matt; he's a mix of embarrassed and proud. I look at Amy, sitting forward in her seat, her elbows on her knees; she's excited for the movie.

The lights dim. The Paramount logo, with its mountain and halo of stars, lights up the screen. Matt leans over and whispers into my ear, "I am so glad you're here, Tretch. Really."

I barely even notice as Jessica Lange drifts up across the screen on a raft.

If I told you that, at some point during the movie, I fell asleep and dreamt I had climbed a skyscraper with a distressed Matt in tow, only to find myself swatting at menacing airplanes painted to look like Amy Sinks, I would be lying.

But only because I didn't fall asleep during the movie . . . even though the citywide struggle to save Jessica Lange from King Kong was nothing compared to the struggle I had keeping my eyes open. I might have let myself go—but not with Matt right there, and the thought of his dads catching me nodding off on their big night.

If I *had* dreamt that—myself climbing a skyscraper with Matt in tow—it's likely that it wouldn't have ended well. I'm not sure if I ever even realized it before, but King Kong dies at the end. And as he falls to his death and lands in a tragic heap, blood and all, and Jessica Lange runs to him, people snapping pictures of her all the while, it occurs to me just how chaotic and mean everything can be at times. It's not a feeling I want to have. It's not something I even want to think about.

"Tretch loved it. He totally cried," Matt tells his dads afterward. He's got a big smile on, so I know he enjoyed it. Ron and Landon are holding hands and also smiling. Amy takes a look at Matt and now she's smiling, too. They're smiling at each other.

"Aw, Tretch," Ron says. "Remember, it's just a movie." We all laugh, and I wipe my eyes a few more times. Eventually, we are the last people in the theater. I really want to get out, though. Switch gears, think about something else.

"Hey," I say, "wasn't there a meteor shower supposed to happen tonight?"

"Oh my *God*, Tretch, you're right!" Matt exclaims. "It was even part of my plan and I forgot. Dad, Pop, I gotta take Amy and Tretch to Picnic Peak. We gotta go now. Oh my God, we might miss it! Come on, we gotta go—"

"Matt, calm down—it's supposed to go until eleven." Landon looks at his watch. "Oh wait, never mind. It's ten thirty. You had better . . ."

"It's *ten thirty*?" Matt pinches my shoulder. "Okay, people, we gotta go. Let's get a move on. Up we go."

Outside the Old Muse, Matt runs ahead of us like he's taken a whiff of some Shakespearean fairy drug. I lag behind.

"Let's go, let's go, Tretch! Come on, it's just uphill!"

Uphill? I think. No one mentioned *uphill*. Amy heaves up behind me and puts her hand on my shoulder. "Good God, Matt!" she calls out. "What is this? Cross-country?"

"You *guuuys*." Matt's begging now. We can see him through some branches, not quite at the "peak" part of Picnic Peak, but already considerably closer than me or Amy. "It's not even that steep!"

"Matt." I prop my foot against the base of the incline. "I feel plenty confident that there will be other meteor showers to witness in this lifetime. And possibly in the next."

"But not *now* you won't," he argues, poking his head out

between some branches. "Not while you're standing right next to your best bud, you won't."

Amy pulls even with me. "Matt's right, Tretch. It will never be the same if it's not now. Let's go!" With that, she hustles on ahead. I feel like I might as well be running bleachers in PE. And to think I believed my dance moves were keeping me in shape.

"*Woooooow!*" Matt exclaims. "Wow! Wow! *Wow!* Amy! Get up here—you gotta see this!"

This kills me.

"I'm almost there, Matt!" she calls.

This kills me harder. Because I'm running now, and I'm almost there, too. Just right behind her, really.

"Come on, come on, come on!" he coaxes.

"I'm here!" she cries. She beat me. God, she beat me to it. He grabs her hand as I summit, and I see—that the whole thing is beautiful. The night sky. A meteor overhead flashing. *Will they lace their fingers? Will they lace their fingers?* They lace their fingers, and I am dead. I have actually died. I saddle up on a meteor and jet straight out the park. Straight out of Warmouth, away from Matt, off the face of this entire plane of reality altogether. *Don't look back*, I command myself. *Don't look back.* I'm being melodramatic. I look back. Their fingers are still laced.

"I'm here," I say.

"God, isn't it beautiful?" he asks, and she responds, "Yes. Yes, it is."

I try to agree, "Sure is," but I'm breathing too heavily. No one can hear a word I say before it evaporates. I try again, "Sure is," but this time it's my body that's evaporated, and I'm suddenly with the meteors. Light like an electric surge spits out across the black sky. It does leave me breathless. I gasp.

Matt turns. "Hey, Tretch!" he calls. "Come over here with us. I swear it's even better from over here."

At this point, a good friend probably shakes his head, says, "No, no, man, I'm good over here" or something, and lets the lovebirds have their moment.

But a not-so-good friend—he runs right over, says, "Oh yeah, you're right, the view's *much* better over here," and stands close enough to his friend that they bump knuckles occasionally. As if on accident.

Now, guess which one I was.

When we come down, Ron and Landon are sitting on a park bench. They are holding hands, too, and for some reason that makes me even sadder.

"You guys ready?" Landon asks, and I say yes all too quickly, quickly enough that it might be rude.

"Okeydoke." Landon stands. "We'll meet you at home, babe," he says to Ron.

"See you, babe," Ron replies. "Tretch, Amy"—he flashes a quiet little smile at us—"I hope to see you both soon."

"Absolutely," Amy says.

"Absolutely," I repeat. I mean, Amy Sinks and I already like the same boy and apparently the same T-shirts. I might as well copy the way she answers questions, too.

Ron heads off toward the overfill parking lot behind the Old Muse, and we head to our spot near the entrance. Matt leans into me and whispers, "Hey, Tretch, do you mind if Amy and I listen to my iPod in the backseat?"

"Uh, well, no, of course not. But why would you rather listen to music when you could be talking?"

"Because I'm nervous. And I'm running out of things to say."

I can't help but smile at that. "Seriously?"

"Totally," he says. "I know. I'm pathetic. But I'm to the point now where, for every worthwhile thing I say, I say like ten stupid things, so . . ."

"Well, what are you even going to listen to?"

"I don't know." He slides the iPod out of his pocket. We are beside the car now. "Who wants shotgun?" Landon asks, and I raise my hand. He pulls the door open, and I slide on in. "Thanks, Mr. Landon."

"No problem, Tretch-o."

Amy opens the door for Matt, and he fumbles with his headphones for a second while trying to buckle his seat belt.

His cheeks get all bright red in the car light. I try to send a vote of confidence his way by looking in the rearview, but Amy pulls the door closed and the light disintegrates before I can.

"You want to listen to some music?" he asks her.

"Sure," she says.

"Just promise you won't judge me for the amount of Taylor Swift. I swear, I download all of that for Tretch. Tretch doesn't have an iPod *or* a phone . . . and, oddly, he isn't Amish."

"Do the Amish especially like Taylor Swift?" Amy jokes.

"If they do, I'm in the wrong religion," I interject, which makes Amy laugh.

But seriously. No one need think my love for Taylor Swift is a joke. It's like some people (Matt) are embarrassed to like Taylor Swift or something. Not me. In fact, if anyone ever stopped me and asked, "Tretch Farm, who would you say is the voice of your generation?" I would say Taylor Swift, hands down, no competition.

"I like Taylor Swift," Landon confesses after all goes quiet in the backseat. I force myself to keep facing forward, to not see how close they're getting. "She's got this one that makes me cry."

"*Really?*" I'm both surprised and not surprised. "Oh wait, let me guess which one. Is it 'Never Grow Up'?"

Landon shakes his head, smiling.

" 'The Best Day'?"

"Is that the one about her mom?"

I nod.

"No," Landon says. "But I do like that one."

"Hmm." I have to think about this. "Okay, those are usually my go-to cry songs. Let's see." I'm riffling through my mental Taylor Swift catalogue. " 'Last Kiss'?"

"Nope."

" 'All Too Well'?"

"Try again."

"Is it older?"

"Yeah, it's an older one."

"Oh my gosh, is it 'Fifteen'? Please tell me it's—"

"That's the one."

"Oh my gosh, *yes*."

"Yep . . . What's the line? Where she's like, in your life, you'll do better things than dating the popular boy, or . . ."

" 'In your life, you'll do things greater than dating the boy on the football team . . . ,' " I recite, pausing in rhythm.

"Yes." Landon nods. "I mean, where was that song when *I* was fifteen?"

"Exactly," I say. "I mean, how did you even survive?"

"What? Being fifteen?"

"Uh, yes." Specifically, I meant being fifteen without Taylor Swift—but if Landon wants to give me the story of his fifteen-year-old self, I'm not complaining.

"Hmm . . . movies, I guess. I went to the movies a lot."

"What movies?"

"Well. When I was growing up, there was an art house cinema only a few blocks away. I used to lie to my mom and tell her I was going to hang out with friends, when really I was just going to the movies."

"Why did you have to lie?"

"I guess I didn't *have* to lie, but I did it mostly just because I didn't want her to feel sad about me going everywhere by myself all the time."

"Oh, I understand."

"Yeah." Landon pauses, reflecting. "That's the theater where I saw *King Kong* for the first time. And a lot of other stuff."

"Oh, cool," I say. "Yeah, that was really neat, what Mr. Ron said about seeing it again with you in college. Is that when y'all met? In college?"

"Yeah," Landon says. "I met him my senior year. Ron was a sophomore."

"And then you got married?"

Landon laughs—actually it's kind of a guffaw, and I don't use the word *guffaw* lightly. "Well, yes, long story short . . . *much* longer story short."

"Can I ask you a personal question?"

"Uh, sure, Tretch."

"Who did the proposing? Was it you or Ron?"

Landon laughs. "You know, oddly enough, no one ever asks that. But I was the one who did the actual proposing."

"Nice," I say. "Where were you guys?"

"We were in a restaurant. This awful Mediterranean restaurant in Queens that smelled like there was some kind of
chemical leak inside it."

"Ooh," I say. "Well, that sounds . . . romantic?"

"Somehow I guess it was. I totally cried throughout the
proposal. Ron cried when he said yes. I'm telling you, it was a
mess." He laughs. "But you know what Ron said to me after
we got ourselves together enough that we could speak? And
you'll get this now that you've seen *King Kong*."

"What?"

"He said, 'Here's to the big one,' and we clinked glasses.
Now how perfect is that?" Landon looks at me and smiles.
Headlights from a passing car light up his face, and his eyes
glisten.

"Pretty perfect," I say, still refusing to look behind me.

In Amy's driveway, she and Matt say their good-byes. It's so
cute. Like, I'm having to watch with one eye closed, it's
so cute.

"Well, bye," he says

"Bye," she says. "See you soon."

"Yeah." He nods. "Thanks for coming."

"Thanks for the invite."

They can't even look each other in the face. She turns
around and jogs up the front steps.

Matt spins in the direction of the car with a massive grin and gives me two thumbs-up. So the night went well. Apparently.

In *my* driveway, Landon turns the headlights off, and Matt taps me on the shoulder. He winks at me from the backseat, and we high-five each other. "Good night," he says, not so much wishing me one as confirming what we just had.

Tonight was a good night.

"Definitely," I agree, unbuckling. "Thanks so much for driving, Mr. Landon."

"You're very welcome, Tretch," he says, winking—gosh, they are the winkingest family. "Great talking to you."

"Yeah, it was for me, too." I sigh, one hand on the roof of the car, the other on the door. "Well, good night, you guys. I'll see you soon."

"Night, Tretch."

"Night, man."

I shut the door then, and they're free to go. I don't look back. I don't look back because that's my rule about good-byes. Once the actual good-bye is said, just keep on walking and don't look back. Because what you do after a good-bye— that's like the punctuation mark at the end of it all, and it can be either a period or a question mark.

My motto: Go for the period. Don't look back. Seal it up, put it away, and there you have it: an entire moment, perfectly packaged, complete.

Landon and Matt back out of the driveway. I don't turn around. I close the front door behind me. I don't turn around.

There's a single light on in the kitchen, the one above the stove, and a sheet of notebook paper on the stove top. I pick it up.

Good night, Tretch!
We tried to wait up for you,
but we got too tired.
Hope King Kong didn't get you!
Love, Mom

Beneath that is a drawing of a vicious King Kong holding a petrified-looking little boy in his fist in Mom's signature drawing style—the one she perfected as head of the comics department for her college newspaper.

Beneath the Kong drawing is another note.

Hey, Tretch. Dad here. Hope your date
went well. Can't wait to hear about it in the
morning. Sorry I didn't get a chance to see
you today. Work's been pretty crazy, or, how
do you and Joe say it, "cray-cray"? Work's
been pretty "cray-cray" lately. Anyway,
good night. Love, Dad

I bust out laughing at the "cray-cray" thing. Dad is pretty "cray-cray" himself.

Beneath that is *another* note—this one from Joe.

> *Hey, Tretch. Just writing to say I hope*
> *your date went well and to point out*
> *that Mom and Dad did not leave*
> *notes for me while I was out.*
> *Therefore, you are the favorite.*
> *I'm off to sleep off my feelings of*
> *inadequacy. Hopefully.*
> *Yours truly, Chopped Liver*

I'm laughing big-time now. Goodness gracious. My entire family is cray-cray, and I kind of freaking love them.

I take the blue pen off the countertop and draw a heart in the only blank space left on the page. Right at the bottom. From the bottom of my heart.

Night, everyone.

six

First full day of break means me sleeping as late as I can, then sticking to my room and my stereo for as long as I can— namely, until hunger gets the best of me and I have to head down to the kitchen. I want some word from Matt, but don't get any—probably because he, too, is riding the first day of break as long as he can.

In all the excitement of the King Kong adventure, I managed to forget about the note Bobby Handel wrote about the two of us. Now I give it some more thought, which is probably more thought than it's worth.

I've been able to recognize Bobby Handel's handwriting

since fifth grade—which was, incidentally, the year he started to pick on me.

The full-on bullying came in the sixth grade, when he just happened to ram me into a locker and then decided it was funny enough to do it Every Single Day after that. He didn't stop doing it for the rest of that year. One day I actually got a cut on my eyebrow from where I hit the corner of the locker next to mine. It had swung open somehow, and I fell into it headfirst after Bobby gave me a good shove.

Bobby saw the blood before I did. In fact, I wouldn't have even noticed it if his face hadn't looked genuinely concerned for a split second. And then he was gone, stomping down the hallway. I put my hand to my face and pulled it away, and sure enough there was a wet, hot red stain.

That was the worst day of the sixth grade, hands down, but Bobby laid off of me for a little while after that, and he's never really *hurt* me again. He still calls me by this stupid nickname I hate: Dancing Queen, after the ABBA song. And the funny thing is: Bobby didn't even come up with that nickname. Nope. That credit actually goes to Mr. *Tim* Handel, Bobby's *dad*.

It all has to do with this time I was working out my choreography to "Physical" by Olivia Newton-John. I had heard the song for the first time on an old *Glee* episode, and it was my favorite at the time, especially since I had some pretty insane moves to go along with it.

Overall, I thought I'd put a pretty good dance together. Sure, *now* I think it was amateur, but for a sixth grader, it wasn't *that* bad. It involved a lot of standard motions like knee bends and hip thrusts and shoulder rolls. There were several fist pumps, even a solitary moment when I flopped down onto my hands and did *one* push-up.

It came together all right.

Then one day, Tim Handel was at the house talking business with Dad. The plumbing downstairs had gone kind of haywire, so he'd had to use the bathroom upstairs. I hadn't shut the door to my room, and when Tim heard the music, he stopped to look in. I was watching my reflection move in the mirror on my closet door, making sure my hip thrusts looked fluid. Tim Handel paused and stood there looking at me with wide eyes. I stopped moving, but too late. He busted out laughing.

"Whatcha doin' there, Dancing Queen?" he asked once he finally caught his breath.

I can't figure out people like Tim and Bobby Handel, so sometimes I think it's best to not even try. Just forget about them and go on about my day.

Which is what I'm trying to do with the note Bobby wrote. If Matt can take it in stride, so can I.

I walk downstairs and smell evergreen-scented candles immediately. It's a make-do smell, considering we haven't bought a tree yet. Mom and Dad and Joe are all so busy. I'm the only one who isn't—I don't think you start to get busy until you can drive. Part of me actually kind of likes it. It makes the time go slower, and I can just take everything in and think about it all.

I thumb through a thin stack of mail sitting on our kitchen counter. A few Christmas cards from Mom and Dad's old college friends, all of them saying things like "Let There Be Peace on Earth!" and "Merry Christmas from Our Family to Yours." The scented candle flickers on the kitchen table.

It used to be that the mail would be sorted and responded to immediately, but Mom's pulling double duty now. She's getting her master's degree in finance because she's ready to move on from her job as secretary at Farm and Handel Insurance, where my dad works. Part of it, I think, has to do with the fact that she's discovering new things about herself, "realizing" her "full potential," as she put it to Joe and me last Friday while she drove us both to buy new jeans. Part of it, I think, has to do with my dad. "Everyone needs a little space," she said. "Even married couples. It's not good for *any* relationship if the two of you stay cooped up in the same place all day long, then come *home* to the same place. We're humans. We need our space like every other species on this earth."

I also think she doesn't enjoy spending that much time up close with Tim Handel. If father is truly like son—and I believe he is—I can't say I blame her.

I wonder now if she's home . . . and then I notice some soft music playing.

Is it? It is.

Celine Dion Christmas.

Mom is definitely home.

I walk into the den, where she's sprawled out on the floor, dead asleep. She hasn't slept much in the past few nights, since she's been having final exams in all her classes. I see some old coffee still sitting in a mug on the coffee table. I pick it up and carry it to the kitchen. I'm washing it out in the sink when I hear her say, "Tretch? That you?"

"Yes, ma'am." I walk into the den, still holding the coffee mug. "You want to start a fresh pot?"

She breathes out, and a strand of her brown hair flutters in front of her face. "Sure," she says. "Might as well."

"Yesterday was the last one, right?" I ask.

"Last one," she says, pumping her fist. "Done. I'm just in recovery mode now." She's still sitting flat on the ground. Her hair's a mess, and she hasn't put on any makeup. But Mom's never been one of those ladies to wear lots of makeup. She has a pretty good natural look all by itself.

"How'd it go?" I ask.

"Oh, it went fine, I think." She holds her hand out and it goes limp. "It better have. I wrote about ten pages."

"*Hoo-wee,*" I say. "Well done."

"Thanks, babe." Mom yawns. In the background, Celine Dion is singing the refrain to "O Come All Ye Faithful." Loudly.

"OHHH COME LET US ADOOOOOORE HIM... OHHH COME LET US ADOOOOOORE HIM ... OHHH COOOOOME LEEEEET UUUS ADOOOOOOORE HIIIIIIM ..."

"Nice music choice," I say.

Mom grins. "Shut up. It soothes me."

We make coffee in the kitchen with the French press. That's how Mom prefers to make it—"cowboy style," she calls it. She tips the press and pours the coffee into two mugs. The dark drink steams. "Tretch, we need a tree," she says.

"I know."

"I mean, Joe's only gonna be here one day to see it, as it is."

Joe is leaving tomorrow for Dallas to go visit Nana and Papa for Christmas. I'm getting the raw end of the deal, with it being too expensive to send both Joe and me, and with it being Joe's turn.

"You'll want to take it easy for a few days after exams, anyways, won't you, Tretch?" she asks, reading my mind, or trying to.

Not really, I think. *I'd rather go to Dallas with Joe and see Nana and Papa than stay in Warmouth and be bored the whole time. Especially since Matt will be gone, too.*

I haven't seen Nana and Papa in about six months now. They mailed me a present for my birthday a month ago.

Mom walks to the pantry and pulls out a few rolls of wrapping paper. "I reckon when Joe gets back from his errands, you and him can go get a tree. I don't know when your dad'll be back. Work's been H-E-double hockey sticks all week."

"I know," I say, "I can tell." Every night recently, Dad's been coming home with this big old red rash creeping out from behind his shirt collar. Pretty soon that thing is going to get so big it'll cover up his whole head, if he doesn't find a way to relax.

I don't understand much about the insurance business, but I know there's a lot of paperwork. And I know paperwork probably gets stressful, just like working next to Tim Handel probably gets annoying.

I sigh. "Dad's like Bob Cratchit," I say.

"Who's that?" Mom asks. She's unspooling some wrapping paper from the roll.

"You know, from *A Christmas Carol*?"

"Not ringing a bell."

I think for a few seconds. "The one Mickey plays in the version with Disney characters."

"*Oh.*" Mom lays out the paper on the kitchen table and seats herself. "Well then, who would be Scrooge?"

"Well," I say. And it seems like the answer is just as obvious. "I guess Dad would be, wouldn't he?"

Mom motions for me to bring her a shoe box with the Nike logo that's sitting on the kitchen counter. "So Dad is both Mickey and Scrooge?"

"Bob Cratchit," I correct. "And yes."

"Now how would that work, Tretch?"

"Well, he's the one getting beat down all the time, like Bob Cratchit." I set the shoe box on the table in front of her. "But, since he's the boss, he's also the one *doing* the beating, like Scrooge."

"What about Tim?" Mom asks.

"Psh," I say. "Tim Handel is *nothing*. No, wait, Tim Handel is like the second ghost. The Ghost of Christmas Present."

"Is that the scary one?" Mom takes a pair of scissors and cuts a large rectangle around the box.

"No. It's the fat one."

"Ah," Mom says, balancing the box, the scissors, the roll of paper, and her coffee cup as she wanders off into her and Dad's bedroom. Mom always acts suspicious and secretive when it comes to wrapping presents. I'm guessing this is wave two, after yesterday.

I hear the front door slam and I know it's Joe before I even look. He walks into the kitchen and pulls the carton of orange juice out of the fridge.

"*Joe!* You want to go get the tree once Dad gets home?"

He pulls off his coat and sets it on top of the counter. "No can do, Tretch-o. Gotta go snag Mom a Christmas present. Then I gotta go say bye to Melissa. I'm not gonna see her again until after Christmas."

"Ah. Gotcha." My shoulders slump. Joe is now taking off a shirt he has layered on top of another one. The top shirt, the one he's pulling off, is purple and has a picture of a brontosaurus on it. *Veg*, it says. That's all.

"You growin' your beard out?" I ask him. That's Joe's and my way of saying to each other, *Hey, you need to shave.*

"Actually, I am," Joe replies.

"Oh . . . Well, did you have a good last day at school yesterday?"

"Sure did." He starts pouring himself a glass of orange juice. "What about you?"

"I did. You want some coffee?"

He eyes me first, then his orange juice. "Nah, I'm good. Are, uh, are you okay, Tretch?"

"Yuh. I just—we made a fresh pot." *That's a lie. Why did I say that? We made it with the French press.* Joe looks at the coffeepot on the kitchen counter, which has old coffee from probably a couple days ago still encircling the bottom of it. It gives the glass walls of the pot a dirty, syrupy kind of look.

"That looks old," Joe says.

"It is." I slap my forehead. "I just remembered. We made it in the French press."

Joe eyes me suspiciously. He takes a couple more swigs of his orange juice. I guess all good older brothers generally know when something is up with their younger sib.

"Tretch," he says, "you want to ride to Target with me?"

Again, I wonder, *What if Joe knows?*

"Yes," I say. "I do."

"Hey, Mom!" Joe shouts. "Tretch and I will be right back!"

"What?" I hear Mom say from the living room. We head out the front door, going down the front steps with the door swinging shut. That's what you have to do in order to buy presents for your mom, I guess: Tell her you're leaving, then shut the door real fast. Otherwise, she'll just ask you where you're going, and that would ruin things.

Joe drives a blue Chevy truck—a '91, I think. It's a piece of junk, but Joe loves it. He loves that it has a tape deck. "Name one person you know who drives a car with a tape deck," he said to me one day.

Truth is, I barely know anyone who drives a car.

Joe turns on the truck and a loud burst of music comes through the radio speakers. *"Eeh-eeh-eeh-eeeeh-eeh . . ."* I've never heard it before, but whatever it is, I dig it.

"What's this?" I ask.

"Uhh . . ." Joe puts the truck in reverse and spins it around, his head turning right and left. "Mixtape Melissa made me. This one is called . . ." He lifts up the plastic case the cassette came in. I can see the white paper insert where Melissa has scrawled the song titles and artist names.

" 'Anything Could Happen,' " Joe says, "by Ellie Goulding."

"Eeh," I sing, echoing the outpouring from the speakers. "I like this beat. Maybe I could do something with it."

"A new dance?" Joe swings his head around and sticks the car in drive.

"I think so. But it'd have to be different than any other one I've ever done. This is kind of *different*." And right now, *different* is awesome. "We taking the highway?"

"Yeah. Bit of a time crunch today."

I nod, a little disappointed. I know Joe really wants to see Melissa before he leaves in the morning. Usually, though, we take back roads wherever we go. It's one of the fun things about living in a small town.

I watch mailboxes whiz by as Joe and I blaze down Watercress Road, then turn left onto the main road.

"Well, I'm bummed you're leaving," I say.

"Yeah, I wish you could go." Joe wipes his nose with his long-sleeve flannel, then reaches for the heat controller on the dash. "I bet next year."

"Yeah," I say. I slide down on the Chevy's cloth seating, until the top of my head touches the bottom of the neck rest.

"So really," Joe says to me, "what's going on?"

I think of Matt, and Matt and Amy, and Bobby Handel's note, and Tim Handel being a total buttface. I think of how all these things have weight, and they're tiring me out. Nobody's going to take the weight off of me. I'm going to have to give it away.

But is this really the right time? Joe's being kind of close-mouthed. But *then* there's the question of whether there will *ever* be a good time. The song coming through the speakers shouts, *"Anything could happen, anything could happen."* I turn the volume down, taking the song as a sign. I've got to make this happen. I need to.

"Joe," I say. "I gotta tell you something."

"Shoot it to me, Tretch."

And then I just say it.

"I'm gay."

It flops out like something I'd been chewing on while trying to speak, and the first thought I have afterward is, *Well, maybe no one noticed*. There's a part of me that hopes Joe still hasn't noticed, hasn't heard. I said it quickly, so fast that I catch even myself off guard. *How weird*, I think. In one quick moment, it's out—and so am I, I guess.

The song on the stereo ends in a tail of *eeh*s, and the cassette stops. I hear the dull knocking of the Chevy's engine, a sound that makes a lot of Joe's less frequent passengers nervous. It makes me nervous now. But not because I'm scared the Chevy will break down.

It makes me nervous because it reminds me of a denting sound, like water pressure pushing in on the walls of a submarine.

We're going down, I think. But then Joe says, "Cool."

That's all he says. I am kind of amazed.

Really amazed, actually.

The next track on Melissa's mixtape begins to unfurl and sound fills the truck again. Joe whistles along. I don't recognize the song playing, but it's some down-tempo acoustic stuff. Not my favorite.

"Thanks for telling me, by the way," he adds.

I swallow. "Well, you're welcome." There's a little water in my eyes, which surprises me because I don't feel like crying. We're on the highway now, a gray sky rolling past us, above us, and, depending on how you look at it, ahead of us, too.

"How hard was that?" he asks. "To tell me."

"Not as bad as I thought," I answer.

Joe gives a short laugh. "Well, good." He pauses, thinking. "Supposedly that's how it goes, actually."

"What do you mean?"

Joe flips the Chevy's blinker on and we merge right, our exit coming up. "I mean, with the whole coming-out deal. Melissa's brother Marcus came out a few years back. He said he always thought it would be a lot worse than it actually is . . . and, you know, Melissa's dad is a preacher."

"I didn't know that," I say. "Wow."

"And you know what he said when Marcus came out to him?"

"What?"

A grin forms on Joe's face. "He said, 'Well, *finally*, Marcus, we were wondering when you were going to tell us.'" Joe chuckles. "That's what he said."

I breathe a kind of raspy laugh, some phlegm caught in my throat. We take a right off of our exit, the Target's red rings suspended and glowing in the distance, higher than the big lighted Christmas ornaments the city hung from its telephone poles, and higher still than the restaurant marquees: a Ryan's, a Golden Corral, a New China Buffet, a Wendy's.

Joe doesn't ask me when I think I might tell Mom and Dad. He doesn't ask about Matt Gooby, or Matt Gooby's dads, or if I'm sure about what I've told him or not: *Sure you're not just confused about all this, Tretch? It can be complicated, you know* . . . Nope. Joe doesn't say anything like any of that. And I love him so much for it right then and there that I can almost tell him so.

Almost.

seven

"So guess what Mom told me you have to do while I'm gone."
Joe is holding a DVD box set of a show called *Charlie's Angels*.
We're standing in an aisle in the entertainment section of
Target. The big TV screens on the wall behind us roar an ad
for a scary movie.

"What?" I ask.

"Feed Spooky," Joe says.

"Are you kidding?" I put down the DVD box set I've been
holding, a season of a show Grandma and Granddad like
called *Hee Haw*. (Earlier, I asked Joe if he thought we should

get it for them, but then he reminded me, "Tretch, they don't even have a DVD player. How would they watch it?")

"I *hate* that cat," I say, and Joe cackles.

"Well, the Whips are going out of town," he says. "They were gonna pay one of us and I was gonna do it, but then I remembered I was going out of town, too."

Spooky is bad luck. I swear, every time I lay eyes on her, something bad happens. That day in the sixth grade when Bobby Handel rammed me into a locker, I had seen her crossing the street on her nasty cat paws, swishing her black tail, on the way to school. And I'd just *known* something bad was going to happen.

It doesn't help that she has a bad attitude on top of that. She acts all superior and doesn't let you pet her or anything. If you try, she will bite you.

"I mean, Joe, we'll *all* be out of town on Christmas and Christmas Eve! We can't feed her on those days!"

"I told the Whips that, but they weren't too concerned. They just said she would catch her a bird or something." Joe puts his hand on his hip and imitates our neighbor Mr. Whip, a really country-sounding man. " 'She'll *have her a right old Christmas feast!*' "

It's pretty dead-on, and pretty hilarious.

The TV screens switch from the scary movie advertisement to something about a boy and a puppy, set somewhere in Alaska. It catches my attention, until I hear this couple fighting nearby. Not *real* fighting or anything, but disputing. Usually I'd think it was just another couple parading their drama in public—call it Target practice—but this time something clicks into place and I realize I recognize one of the voices.

"You hear that?" I whisper to Joe.

He raises an eyebrow. "Yes."

Tim Handel, Dad's business partner and long-time friend, the father of the kid who consistently tries to make my life a living Hades, is fighting with his wife, Sandy, one row over.

Tim and his first wife, Mariana, were the reason my parents met. Mom and Dad were both in the Handels' wedding party. Mom was friends with Mrs. Mariana from college, so she was a bridesmaid. Dad was Tim's best man.

When Bobby and I were five years old, Mariana got sick. Really sick. *Cancer* sick. I remember stopping off with Mom at the hospital in Samsanuk to see her. It's a quick flash of a memory, since I was so young. But Bobby's mom was in the hospital bed, and she didn't have hair—I remember that, and I remember Mom holding my hand. I don't remember talking, or what we did. I just remember it like a picture, quiet and with no movement, Mrs. Mariana's quick warm smile frozen for all time, and that's it.

Mariana died not long after she was diagnosed. It was fast, my mom said, and Tim didn't know what to do, with Bobby being so young. He married Sandy a couple years later, and he and my dad started Farm and Handel Insurance. Every year they give a scholarship to a graduating high school student in honor of Mariana.

A lot of people in town think Tim Handel is a nice guy, just like they think Bobby is such a nice boy. These are the people who don't know the Handel men very well.

Right now, Tim's voice is raised in a loud whisper. "We just can't afford that!"

"What do you mean? How can we not?" Sandy shoots back.

Uh-oh. I look at Joe. If the Handels are having financial problems, it most likely means *we're* having financial problems as well. Joe squints his eyes like he's really curious now.

"We have—" Tim sighs. "We have *enough*, Sandy. We just can't afford to—"

"To what, Tim?"

"To give him everything he wants." Tim sighs again, a big one this time. "His grades are bad and he's getting in trouble more. We shouldn't feed that kind of behavior—"

"I know, but, my God, Tim. It's Christmas—"

Joe and I are so absorbed in overhearing that we don't realize the Handels are rounding the corner until it's too late.

I don't know what to do. So I leave that up to Joe.

"Well, hey, y'all," he says as the Handels spot us. "What's up?"

"Well, what do you know, it's the Farm boys," Sandy says. She comes up to us and puts a hand on Joe's arm and a hand on mine. "Doing some shopping?"

"Yeah," Joe says, showing her the DVD set. "For Mom."

"Oh, she'll *love* this. There isn't a woman I know who grew up in our time who doesn't miss watching that show. You see this, Tim?"

He nods and smiles in a pained way. Tim Handel is big, round, and clean-shaven. He wears khaki pants all the time. His hair is cut short, military style, and pepper-colored. He has a rough face, too—he's not the kind of guy you would say looks friendly. But when he smiles, I guess he looks friendly enough. "I see it," he says. "You boys glad to be out of school?"

"We are," I answer and, wanting to sound friendly, add, "I know Bobby is, too." At my mention of Bobby, his nod is thrown off a beat—I've surprised him. I wonder if Mrs. Cook called him about the note in class. Or if he just thinks it's weird that a loser like me would presume to know what's going on in the head of a jerk like his son.

Sandy chirps in with a "Yes, I know *all* you boys are glad to be out." She widens her smile so it can block any other thoughts from being expressed. "Well, have a merry Christmas, you two. Tell the folks hi!"

I look at Joe once they're gone. "*Whoops*," I say.

"Yeah, whoops."

"Probably shouldn't have brought up Bobby."

"Probably not."

We continue shopping without incident. We tease and trash-talk and joke with each other just like we always have. I guess a part of me was afraid that me being gay would alter that, would make him retreat a little, or—even worse—make him pretend that everything was cool while retreating at the same time. But there's no apparent sign of retreat, no pretend. And I am so grateful for that.

When we get back to our house, I'm expecting Joe to come in with me. Then I remember he's going to see Melissa.

"Well, Tretch," he says, "I wish I was gonna be able to go get the tree with you guys."

"Yeah," I say, sliding from the passenger seat. "It's no big."

I almost add something like *There's always next year, anyways*, but then I remember: *college*. I don't know what Joe will be around for next year.

"But you and Dad have fun," he tells me.

I start to get out of the car, but Joe interrupts me with one more thing. "Oh, and, Tretch—thanks for telling me about . . . you know."

I look him in the eye. "Thanks for . . . well, thanks for being so cool."

Joe nods, and a beat goes by where we don't say anything.

I snap my fingers. "*Ooh*—I just remembered. Did you and Melissa see the meteor shower last night? It was suuuuper romantic."

Joe snorts and shakes his head. "You are the *biggest* doofus, you know that?"

"Proudly," I say. Then I shut the door to the Chevy and walk up the driveway to the house. When I get there, the door swings open. Dad steps out and nods at me quickly.

"Where's Joe going?" he asks. I notice the red rash on his neck. It doesn't look bad today, not as bad as yesterday. Maybe his stress has shrunk a little.

"Melissa's," I answer. "He wants to tell her bye."

"He get your mom a present?"

"Yes, sir."

"He's not going to pick out the tree with us?"

"I—" I turn around, like I expect Joe to be pulling back up the driveway after changing his mind. "I don't think so, Dad."

Dad looks hard down the driveway. It's a stare I know Joe has to feel, even though he's probably to the end of Watercress Road by now. "Welp," Dad says, "guess it's just me and you, then." He starts down the front porch steps.

"Okay," I say. "I just gotta put—" The *Charlie's Angels* DVD collection is tucked inside my jacket. I wanted to sneak it in without Mom knowing and hide it under my bed.

"Don't go in there," Dad warns. "Your mom's ticked."

"About what?"

Dad shrugs.

"Oh," I say. "Well, okay." I follow him down the porch steps, and he disappears into the garage. I look across the street and spot Spooky's tail waving from the Whips' front lawn.

"Nasty old cat," I say.

"Here, Tretch, hold on to this, will you?" Dad pushes a long handsaw into my hands. "Hold it tight." He opens the passenger door to the Honda Accord for me, and I slide in.

"Okay."

The saw remains on my lap the whole trip. For the duration, I live in fear of what would happen if we stopped short. Finally, we pass a sign that reads, HUCKABEE'S TREES: CUT 'EM YOURSELF AND IT'S FREE! 3 MILES.

"Can't beat Huckabee's," I say in my local-country-TV-commercial voice.

"That kind of business could only ever work in a small town," Dad grunts. "And it won't work that way much longer. Not even in small towns like Warmouth."

I try balancing the saw between my legs. It makes an eerie, wobbly sound every time Dad turns the wheel.

"So what was up with Mom?" I ask.

Dad scratches his neck. "Just all this holiday stuff. Trying to get presents for everyone and all that." He tugs at his collar, revealing more irritated skin. "She's trying to figure out what we're going to get the Handels, for Christ's—uh, for crying out loud."

"Why do we have to get the Handels anything?"

"Exactly!" Dad blurts. Then he calms down. "I mean, I get it. I get why it's important to your mom. After all, Mariana was—"

"Her best friend."

"Right. Which reminds me—you remember that vase that used to sit on the coffee table in the living room?"

Oh, God. I gulp. "Yes, sir."

"Any idea where that went? It's not there anymore. Your mom was wondering about it today."

"Beats me." Since I never lie, he believes me. Or at least it looks like he believes me.

"Well, she was asking about it." Dad clears his throat. "You know, that was the gift Tim gave us the first Christmas after Mariana died."

"*Oh.*" I didn't know.

"Yeah." He looks straight ahead, tapping the steering wheel to the beat of the Christmas song on the radio. "Ha."

"What?"

Dad shakes his head. "I guess, now that I think about it— it's really all because of that Christmas that we even still *exchange* gifts with the Handels."

"What do you mean?"

"Well, Tim and I never exchanged a gift between the two of us our whole lives. I mean, I'm sure Mom and Mariana did. Girls care about that stuff. But Tim brought that vase over the day after Christmas the year Mariana passed away. She died in September. I don't know if you remember—"

That frozen image pops back into my mind. "I only remember a little bit," I say.

"Yeah, well, Tim brought that vase over the day after

Christmas. It had a ribbon wrapped around it and everything, and he said, 'Can you believe I almost forgot? Mariana would have killed me.' He had Bobby with him. Gosh, how old were you guys then?"

"Five."

"Yeah, poor kid. He was so little. I don't even think he understood—"

"I'm sure he didn't," I say. And, for a second, I try to picture life without Mom. But I can only really let myself get to the edge of the idea. I don't want to know, don't want to know if it's even possible *to* know—

"Poor kid," Dad says again. And I think, *Yeah, poor kid.* It doesn't excuse who he's become. But it's still sad.

We roll to a stop, the headlights glinting off a silver metal gate. A chain holds it fast against a wooden fence post.

"I'll get it," I say, opening the car door. I lay the saw flat on my seat as I stand. The cold air pulses against my ears. I hustle over, undo the chain, and pull open the gate.

"Hope we don't scare old Mrs. Huckabee," Dad says once I've closed the gate and hopped back in the passenger seat. He parks the Accord next to a medium-size evergreen. It's a bit crooked, maybe, but Dad says it will do.

"Let's just get it quick and get home," he tells me. "It's *freezing* out here." I drag the saw out behind me and pass it to him. He kneels on the ground and saws away for what can't be longer than two or three minutes. The evergreen tilts suddenly, sprinkling bristles on the ground. "Tim-berrr!" I holler, really just because I want to.

Dad stands, tipping the tree the rest of the way with his foot. He looks at me. "Tim-*burrr*!" he says, making his teeth chatter. "All right, Tretch, bring me those bungee cords from the trunk."

I do what I can to help tether the tree to the roof of the Accord, which isn't a whole lot. Mostly, I just stand to the side and ask Dad things like "Won't it scratch the paint?" and "What do you plan to hook the bungee cords to?" But he doesn't seem to mind. I think he likes the company, honestly. I think Dad always likes to have company, and I think his favorite company, for the most part, is Mom and Joe and me.

For a second, I imagine having the same conversation with him that I had with Joe.

But there's no way it would be the same conversation. Ever.

"What time did Joe say he's going to be home tonight?" Dad asks when we're back in the car.

I shrug. "He didn't say."

Instead of taking the conversation anywhere else, I stare out the window the whole drive home.

eight

One morning last year, in the locker room after PE, Bobby Handel came up to me holding a toothbrush.

Stupidly, I thought he was going to brush his teeth.

Instead he reached out, grabbed the waistband of my shorts, pulled it, and dropped the toothbrush down my front. The band of my shorts snapped back with a *foomp!*

"Hey, look, everyone!" Bobby proclaimed. "Farm has got a hard-on!"

Some guys chuckled, but for the most part I don't think anyone thought it was really that funny. Especially not Matt.

"Back up, Handel," he said, coming over as I fished the toothbrush out and dropped it. It bounced off my blue Nike and onto the tile locker room floor. "Lay off for once."

"*Ooh,*" Bobby taunted. "Gayby's standing up for his *boyfriend.*"

I wanted to disappear. But Matt stayed strong.

"Shut up, Handel," he said. "Everyone knows using gay slurs is the number one tactic closet cases use to hide themselves."

"Hm," Bobby said, smiling. "I bet your dads told you that, didn't they, Gayby?"

Matt relaxed his shoulders. "As a matter of fact, they did."

As he grabbed me by my shoulder, I knew I was going to cry. I heard shower knobs turn and running water stop.

"Come on, Tretch," Matt said. He led me out of the locker room and pulled me into the equipment closet. I cried then. I cried right into Matt's shoulder. "It's okay, man," he whispered. He rubbed my back. "It's okay."

I'm thinking about this because it's been almost two whole days and I haven't heard anything new from Matt. I'm thinking about this because Bobby Handel is never going away. And I'm thinking about this because right now I'm wrapping a motorized toothbrush for my cousin Janie. It's one of those toothbrushes that plays a Justin Bieber song when you press the button. Janie's only six, and she's my second cousin, so I guess that means a motorized toothbrush is an okay Christmas gift. Still, I look at my mom with my eyebrows raised.

"What is *this*?" I ask.

"Janie wanted it," Mom tells me. "I swear. Not my idea." She crosses her heart and loosens the collar of her Christmas sweater. It's bright red with some sparkles on it and two reindeer—one with *Joe* stitched over it and one with the name Richie. Mom had it made the Christmas after I was born, and my reindeer, the Richie one, has a bright red nose.

I press the button on the toothbrush. *"Baby, baby, baby, ooooh,"* it sings. I wince, then wrap it in green tissue paper and bury it in a bag with a string handle. "Here ya, go, Mom," I say, handing it over.

"Thank you, thank you," she half says, half sings. She's putting all the presents for our Dallas relatives into a gigantic suitcase.

"Don't you ever miss Nana and Papa at Christmas?" I ask.

"It's not that bad. I'm glad Joe's going for a couple days, at least, so he can get these presents to them." She zips up the suitcase, which is roughly the size of a gator and requires the same kind of wrestling to get its mouth shut. "Christmas was never really a *huge* deal for us. Not like it is with Grandma and Granddad."

"Ah." I nod. It's true, Grandma and Granddad *love* Christmas. In fact, it's hard to imagine two people who love it more. The food, the gifts, the crazy traditions like gingerbread-house-building competitions—they love it all. For the gingerbread-house-building competitions, you can even win a prize, usually some kind of gift certificate scrawled on a scrap of paper in Grandma's hand (*One French Toast Breakfast, Redeemable: Forever*), or a little cartoon penned by Granddad.

"Christmas is a better time with Grandma and Granddad," Mom says.

"You think Joe will have fun in Dallas?"

"They'll probably go ice-skating and stuff, but he'll be glad when it's Christmas Eve and he's coming home. He'll get bored." She looks at me sympathetically. "You're not sad to be staying behind, are you?"

"Nah," I say. But maybe I am a little bit. As a family, we only ever see Nana and Papa once a year, usually at Thanksgiving, and they missed it this year while they were traveling in Thailand. ("They're wanting to see the world in their old age, I guess," Mom had said.)

We had Thanksgiving on Farm Farm instead. Granddad fried up a turkey, and I helped Grandma make some cranberry sauce that was actually good. Still, it was only a prelude to Christmas—because at Christmastime on Farm Farm, we *really* feast.

We start on Christmas Eve with the Spaghetti Casserole Feast for lunch. It's a good start but never the biggest. Then we have the Christmas Eve Feast, which is *enormous*. There's usually a ham and a turkey (turkey because Grandma says it will help Joe and me get to sleep on Christmas Eve night, something that used to be hard when we'd be too excited), some of Grandma's famous dressing, sweet potatoes, green beans, hash-brown casserole, squash, peas, usually something leafy like collards or turnip greens—and more.

Yeah, I think, *Joe will definitely be happy to be back home before Christmas*. Right now, he's packing in his room. I know he's done when I hear him tip over his suitcase at the top of the stairs.

"*All riiiight*," he sings, dragging it behind him, making it thump with each step. "I'm ready to make this yuletide gay!"

He looks right at me, smiling, and I respond by shooting him daggers. *Don't push it, Joe*, I want to say. I look over to Mom and am relieved to see she doesn't suspect a thing.

"I can't believe you're missing the tree lighting," I say. "All for a measly Dallas trip? I mean, come *on*, man." I roll my eyes.

"Yeah, you're right. The Warmouth Christmas tree-lighting ceremony is *waaaay* cooler than Dallas, Texas, right? I mean, every metropolis in the *world* is jealous of what Warmouth does at Christmas. It's like Jesus was born just so, two thousand years later, Warmouth could slap some lights up on a pine."

"Don't speak that sacrilege!" Mom warns from the kitchen. "Plus, you both used to *love* the tree-lighting ceremony!"

Joe winks at me. "Well, it *is* a treasured Warmouth tradition."

Mom stomps into the living room. A grocery bag swings from her wrist, filled with airplane snacks for Joe. "It *is* a treasured Warmouth tradition, and you know you love it," she says. "Tretch, help Joe carry all this stuff out to the car."

I grab the present-filled suitcase and lug it to the front door. I turn to catch Mom kissing Joe on the forehead. "Be safe," she says.

"I will."

"And I mean safe."

"Mom, it's not like I'll be flying the plane."

"Safe."

"Yes! Okay! I promise!" He says. Then he turns to me. "Tretch, sing your heart out tonight." He cracks another smile.

"Shut up," I say. With Joe gone, I will be the only guy in the Warmouth Methodist Choir tonight, performing "Silent Night" at the tree-lighting ceremony.

He walks by me, humming "Silent Night" and giving me a soft sock to the shoulder. I pick up the suitcase full of presents and load it into the back of the Chevy.

"Heavy," I say.

"Fragile," Mom says, walking up behind me. She kisses Joe on the cheek. "I love you."

"I love you, too." Joe hugs her for as long as she needs. "See ya, Tretch."

"See ya, Joe. Have fun." We hug really fast.

"*Allllllrighty*, then," he says, putting a period on things. He gives Mom and me one last look. "Well, I'll see y'all Christmas Eve." He hops in the truck, swings the door shut, and backs down the driveway. Then he looks back at us and gives one last wave before turning onto the street.

He's off—and I'm left alone again with my secret . . . and the Warmouth United Methodist Church Choir.

Oh holy night.

The key to not being heard as the one male in an otherwise female choir is to sing as high and as quietly as possible. Unless, of course, you can just mouth the words—which I try to do at the tree-lighting ceremony, until Mom catches me and elbows me in the ribs. Beside me, she is belting her heart out while simultaneously giving me what Joe and I call "the eyes," which is when she makes her eyes go all big, quite scarily. This time it's even scarier, because it's in the middle of the "hoooooly" part of "Silent Night," so her mouth is in a big O shape. She looks like a sinister owl.

I open my mouth and sing sharply. "*Allllllll is caaaalm, alllllll is bright.*" *Oof*, I think, *too high.* I try dropping an octave for the next line. "*Rooooouuund yon viiiirgin*"—my deep loud croak smashes through the choir ladies' tinkling harmonies like a testosterone sledgehammer, and Mom gives me the eyes again. I don't even have to turn my head this time. I know. I gulp. Back to mouthing.

After "Silent Night" finally falls silent, I step down off the risers.

"Tretch," Mom says, holding out her hand to me. The choir robes are pretty easy to trip over, so I help her off the riser. The lighted courthouse lingers behind us, the dark Christmas tree perches up ahead, and in between there's a crowd of people shuffling around folding chairs and food stations.

I spot a card table where Amy Sinks is doling out Mabel's hot chocolate. I wave across the lawn and call out, "Hey, Amy!" She waves back. I look to see if Matt's with her, but he's not.

"Ooh, Tretch, she is such a cutie," Mom says into my ear.

"Mom, remember. That's Matt's girl."

I have no idea where this phrase comes from, or whether or not it's true. It's something I'm saying to shut her up, but it has the opposite effect: It shuts me up instead.

"Aha." Mom nods. I have no idea what she's doing with this information.

"I'm gonna go talk to her," I say.

"Okeydoke. I'll go find Dad." Mom does an about-face and marches across the courthouse lawn. I spot Dad off at a corner table that has a decorate-your-own-sugar-cookie stand. He's dumping green sprinkles over a slather of cream cheese icing.

I go over to the hot chocolate stand. "Tretch," Amy says when I get there. "Good singing, man!"

"Ah, thanks, Amy."

"You want some hot chocolate?"

"Yes, please."

She hands me a paper cup with a cloud of steam over it, her gloved hands wrapped around it as she passes it off. I notice her gloves match her hat.

"Hey, you seen Matt?" she asks.

"Huh?" I reply. "Oh, no, no. He usually doesn't come to these things." I take a sip of the hot chocolate.

"Oh." Amy rubs some wetness on her gloves against her apron. "Well, I could've sworn I saw him earlier . . ."

"TRETCH!"

His voice comes from behind me.

Oh God, I think. *Why would he come?*

I turn and call out his name.

He saw me singing. He saw me singing with the Warmouth Methodist Church Choir.

Matt crosses over from a table passing out hot sausages. "Great singing, dude!" He puts a hand on my shoulder. Matt with his shining face and deep green eyes, his bushy wintertime hair. I vaguely hear the countdown as the crowd shouts, "Five . . . four . . . three . . . two . . . one . . . MERRY CHRISTMAS!" and someone somewhere flips a switch. The

Warmouth Christmas tree explodes in bright gold light. I see it reflected in Matt's eyes.

"I didn't know you were in the *choir*!" he says to me, smiling.

I laugh. "Uh, yeah. Something my mom likes me to do."

"Cool, man!" He's looking past me now at Amy. *So, she's the real reason*, I think. *She's the real reason he came.* He waves bashfully. I don't know why he's still acting shy.

Amy says hi and hands him a cup of hot chocolate. He smiles and takes a swig. "Mmm," he says when he pulls the cup back. "Mabel's finest."

I think I should make like the steam coming from the hot chocolate and evaporate into thin air—but then Matt gives me the surprise of my life by turning back to me and asking me if I want to sleep over.

Uh, let me think about my answer for a second . . .

YEEEEEESSSSSSS!

Somehow I manage a calm but still excited-sounding "Of course!" Then I realize I'm going to need permission in order to do this. I spot Mom and Dad across the lawn at a table where the Ladies Auxiliary is handing out eggnog. Spiked eggnog.

"I'll be right back—I'm just going to make sure it's okay," I tell Matt, trying my hardest not to act like this is all I want for Christmas.

"I'll be here," Matt says, using it as an excuse to touch Amy's shoulder.

But I don't dwell on this. I have better things to think about.

"Dad! Mom!" I approach them from behind while they drink nog and talk to our pastor, Reverend Greene, and her husband. I like Reverend Greene a lot, and not just because she has blond bouffant hair like Dolly Parton.

Reverend Greene is the first of them to see me. "Well, hey, Tretch!" she says, holding her own cup of nog. "How is everything?"

"Hey, Reverend Greene. Everything's going good."

"Happy to hear it." Her face looks like polished porcelain. Dad says she must be at least sixty, but I don't believe it. Her husband, whom we just call Mr. Greene, shakes my hand and gives a polite "Greetings."

"What's up?" Dad asks, already pink-faced from the nog.

It wasn't really part of my plan to ask permission to stay over at the Warmouth gay couple's house for the night while standing directly in front of a preacher. But it'll call more attention if I try to pull them aside, so I decide to just go for it.

"Mind if I stay over at Matt's tonight?"

It's not like I'm expecting shrieks of horror. More like a polite excuse to make the problem go away.

Mom steps up next to me and puts her arm around my neck. "Well, of course you can, Tretch!" She squeezes the fabric of my sleeve around my shoulder. "It's spring break! I mean, winter break, after all!"

Dad grins, red-faced. "Have fun, Tretch. Y'all gonna walk there?"

"Yes, sir," I say.

"All right. Just give a call before you're settled in."

"Will do."

"Love ya, Tretch."

"Love you, too, Dad."

"Love ya, Tretch!"

"Love you, too, Mom." I laugh, and my smile meets up with Reverend Greene's.

"It's nice to see you, Tretch," she says. "You were really good in the choir tonight."

"Thanks so much, Reverend Greene!" I say. "Nice to see you, too!"

It feels like I just drank a gallon of spiked nog. Or maybe just the spiked part, not the nog. As I return to Matt, there's a celebration sprouting up inside of me, like an illumination of ten thousand Christmas-tree lights, all neon and golden. I honestly have to stifle a skip. I'm that happy.

Back at the hot chocolate table, I practically shout, "Matt! I can *stay*! I can stay over!"

"Good deal, man," he says. We high-five. "Okay, let's *go*! Amy, you coming?"

Wait. What?

"Yeah," she says. And it kills me, because she looks excited, too. "I just gotta push this cart down to Mabel's and stick it in the kitchen." She starts to pick up the half-empty percolator, and Matt steps over to help her. "Thanks," she says as he takes his place at the back of the cart, offering to push. Amy places a hand on the cart. "We'll push it together," she says.

"Need me to push, too?" I ask.

"We need your moral support," Amy answers. "Stay close!"

I follow them down the sidewalk. They chatter and chatter and occasionally toss back a question to me.

From Matt: "So, Tretch, do you *like* singing in the choir?"

"Oh," I say. "Yeah, sometimes."

From Amy: "Okay, singing or dancing? What do you like more?"

I snort. "About equal, I guess." I know I'm being a drag. I know I should knock it off and loosen up. I watch my steps on the sidewalk, missing each crack, and think, *Okay, get a grip, because there is no reason for you to be like this. All you should be right now is happy.* The door to Jim Cho's, where families are getting Chinese takeout and hanging around long enough for their kids to tell Santa what they want, is open. Some paper napkins float down the sidewalk in the cold air, along with some more paper trash. I catch a glimpse of red ink on one tiny, tiny scrap of paper and pick it up. A fortune.

YOU WILL ALWAYS BE SURROUNDED BY
GOOD FRIENDS.
LUCKY #S: 1, 23, 10, 34, 49, 35

"Oh, cool," I say.

"What you got there, Tretch?" Matt halts the cart, and he and Amy turn to me.

"From a fortune cookie," I say. I read it aloud to them.

"Hoo-wee!" Matt whoops like a cowboy. "Good fortune!"

We continue past Jim Cho's, Christmas music drifting out the open door on a tide of polite talking and children's voices. Inside the restaurant, everything has a festive, bright red feel. Part of that is because of the lighting in Jim Cho's, which is always kind of low, and the rust-colored walls. But everybody inside looks joyful. Parents and young kids alike, all rosy-cheeked and smiling. The Jim Cho's Santa Claus is doing his laugh, Jim Cho shouting, "Say cheese!" and kids responding, "Cheeeeeeese!" We don't stop for long, but it's enough for me to feel festive again. *Just chill out, Tretch, it's a good night.* I step up beside Matt as he and Amy push the cart down the remainder of the sidewalk, Mabel's on the corner up ahead.

Amy lets us into the kitchen with her staff key, and Matt and I hoist the cart up over the threshold. He nudges it inside, and we leave it there.

"Mabel said she would wash it out tomorrow," Amy says. We step outside, and she locks the door again. Matt looks at me and smiles. "Cold," he says, and blows out a big cloud of breath. Amy steps beside him and blows a cloud of her own into it.

Watching this could break my heart a little bit. But I won't let it. Instead, I blow a little fog of my own into their cloud. They don't seem to mind, or even really notice.

Amy grins. "Y'all ever been on the roof?"

This is one of those cool high school things Matt and I haven't done yet. But all it takes is a climb up the two-story fire escape, with Amy in the lead.

At the top, we look over the edge, down at the street not too far below. We are above the streetlights, so we're in no danger of being seen. People are filtering out of Jim Cho's, and slowly the noise is dying, everyone heading home to hit the sack. The courthouse at the end of the street has turned off its lights, but the Christmas tree shines bright. I think about my parents, about how funny tonight is shaping up to be. The festive lights make a kind of haze along the tops of the stores. It's like Barrow Street is right below heaven or something, and Matt and Amy and I are right above it.

"This is great," Matt says.

"Yep yep." Amy nods. "And now you're cool."

"For real," I say.

We stay up there and watch as Jim Cho's shuts down for the night. The lights inside switch off, and we even see the lonely Jim Cho himself, the last man to leave, amble down the street to his car.

"Wonder where the Jim Cho's Santa sleeps?" Matt says. Amy makes a closed-mouth *I don't know* sound, and we stand there waiting to see if the Jim Cho's Santa emerges. It doesn't appear that he's going to.

My hands are cold, so I slide them into the pockets of my jeans, eyeing Matt's pockets as I do, picturing what it would be like to slide my hands into them, an imaginary moment where he allows it, welcomes it even. No Amy Sinks, just him and me, my hands flattened, passing over the terrain of his hips, the front of his thighs, and finally in between. *Rooftop, through-the-pocket hand job. Is that even possible?* But that's as far as I'll allow myself to go for now. I take my hands from my pockets and cup them together, doing my best to ignore the feathery feeling at the tip of my semi-hard as it tests the bounds of my underwear.

Luckily (I guess), Matt and Amy's shoulders are touching, which is a boner kill. They are leaning into each other, smiling little warm smiles of contentment. I can tell they're both feeling it. "What time is it?" I ask.

Matt checks his phone. "Eleven fifteen," he announces, and Amy says, "Hmm. Well, guys, it's been fun." She nudges Matt's shoulder. They're already acting like a couple.

"Time to go home?" I ask.

"Yeah," Amy says. "Curfew's eleven thirty."

"Alrighty, then," Matt says. "We better split."

I'm the first to the ledge. I sling my leg over and land on the fire escape. I start down and turn when I hear Amy say "Thanks." Matt is holding her hand. I see it brush his shoulder as she steps down. "Whoops," she says. "Hair."

He laughs, bashful. And the grin on Matt's face is something special. I whisper "I love you" as they climb down, and I'm not exactly sure if I'm saying it directly to Matt or if I'm putting the words into her mouth and speaking them for her. But I see happiness there. I see happiness I want so badly, and while he holds her arm as they make their way down, whispering things that cause her to laugh, I think, *Amy Sinks, you stole him*, even though I know that's not true. It's not like I've ever even had a shot, but still—

Maybe, in my head, I thought that it might someday be possible.

And I might, in my head, somehow still believe that it is.

So I'm sorry, Amy and Matt, if I can't really want this for the two of you. Matt hops the last few steps and spins around to face her. "Ta-da!" he calls out, the magician of the moment. *But just know that I will try. I will sure as hell try.* "We better run! I'm gonna be late!" Amy jumps off and starts down the alley.

"Come on, Tretch!" Matt calls.

We take off down deserted Barrow Street. And, again, I get the feeling like someone has turned on the switch in me to light me up. I wonder if that's how Matt and Amy would describe it, too. That feeling.

Matt gets that crazy look in his eyes and hops onto a bench, pulling Amy up with him, then the two of them pulling me up next. We all teeter there, trying to balance, and we're *laughing*. I'm laughing so hard my eyes sting. When we finally hop down, we take turns swinging around lampposts. *These are friends*, I think. *These are my friends*. At the edge of the courthouse, we climb the William Griggers statue.

"Good *evening*, Sir Griggers!" Matt says, swinging from the memorial's stone shoulder. We all hang on by an arm and hand, one leg suspended. "*Merry Christmas!*" Matt yells. "*Merry Christmas, Warmouth!*"

"*Merry Christmas, Warmouth!*" I chime in.

"*Merry Christmas, Warmouth!*" Amy thirds.

Then we all just shout out whatever comes to us.

"*Ha-ha! Old fart town!*"

"*Sleepy old town!*"

"*Wake up, Warmouth!*"

"*Wake up, Warmouth!*"

"*Wake up!*"

Somewhere a dog barks.

"*Go to sleep, puppy!*"

We swing down from William Griggers and run some more. "I feel great," Matt says when we reach the corner of Barrow Street. "I feel really, really great."

Amy's house is only a block away. We walk her to the mailbox. I'm about to say good-bye when she leans in and kisses

Matt. It doesn't last long, but it definitely lasts. When they pull apart, they're even brighter than before.

Amy comes over and gives me a hug. "Bye, Tretch!" she says.

"See ya." I pat her shoulder.

She looks at Matt one last time and smiles—"Well, I'd better scoot"—and runs up her driveway. He keeps watching as she disappears inside the garage.

We stay outside until we see the kitchen light in Amy's house flip on, then off, and finally see a light on the second story turn on.

"Her bedroom," Matt says reverently. "Must be."

"Yeah," I say, like a bedroom's no big deal.

We start the walk to Matt's house, moving quickly with big steps, like we've both just realized how cold it is.

It's just the two of us, I think. Now if I can just manage to make it feel like *one more than one* instead of *one less than three*.

nine

Matt is undressing in front of his bedroom mirror while I try not to look.

"I'm so glad your parents actually let you stay tonight," he says. A button unsnaps. A zipper unzips. Pants go sliding.

"Uh, yeah. All thanks to the Ladies Auxiliary eggnog, I guess." I smile at the wall opposite Matt. *My safe wall*, I think. *Nothing suggestive here.* Not unless you count an old poster for the movie *Dune.*

"I think Amy thinks we're cool, man. I really do."

More fabric sliding this time. The underwear, I'm sure. *Why does he do this to me?* "You think?" I ask. "Both of us?"

"Oh yeah, dude! I'm sure. Why else would she have invited us to her party?"

"She invited us to her party?"

"Yeah, dude! New Year's party! Over at Sinks's Young-'n-Fit . . . Oh, by the way, little secret . . ." Matt takes an audible step forward, a slight creak in the floorboard—it's like the soundtrack to the hard-on I'm getting. "Amy's friends with Lana Kramer, and she says Lana's *totally* into you! *And* Amy says she wants to bring you to the party as, like, a date!"

I turn my head (reflex, I swear), and there he is, standing (totally naked, oh my God, oh my God), his hands resting confidently on his waist, as if he's saying, *Hello, world! Here is my penis!*

"Uh, I, uh—" My eyes close, and it's like they're communicating, a tin-can telephone conversation with my brain as the connecting string.

The left eye: *That's big, am I right?*

The right eye: *Yep, I'd say so.*

"Hmm." I press my fist hard against my forehead, a plea for silence. "To tell you the truth, I figured she kind of liked me, but—"

"But *what*?" Matt says, another short step forward. The eyes open; I look up. *Above the waist, Tretch, above the waist.* But above the waist is nice, too.

"I just . . . I mean, I didn't even realize she and Amy were friends."

"Well, sure they are! Why wouldn't they be? And, plus, you love to read, and so does she." Matt argues this like it seals the deal for sure.

"Well, in that case," I say, "bring on the marriage license."

This challenges him. His bare shoulders slump. "*Why*, Tretch?" he says. "Why not at least *try*?"

"She's not my type, Matt."

"Well, what the hell is, then?"

You are! "I don't know." I shrug. "Not yet, anyway."

"How can you not know?" Matt asks. He turns. A slight swaying from his groin area sends out shock waves to mine.

I can't help but look at his butt as he steps inside the bathroom.

"I mean, are you going as *Amy's* date?" I call. I can't follow him in there. I can't even stand—not as long as there's a chance that he'll pop back into the bedroom.

"*Yuh!*" he shouts. The surge of the water stream chirps into life. "Hope so, anyway!" There's the rattle of the curtain, and the squeaking sound of feet on the tub floor.

Now that Matt's in the shower, I'm safe to stand. I sidle out to the hall and tiptoe down the stairs. Ron and Landon were asleep when Matt and I got back. I was honestly pretty sad about that. I wanted to talk to them. But I certainly don't want to wake them now.

I flip on the light in the kitchen and look around. There's a nice kitchen table, speckled granite countertops. A row of cookbooks next to a fancy-looking coffeemaker and a painting of a chicken on the wall. Some clean white wooden cabinets. I see Matt's bicep flexing as he reaches for a coffee mug. *"You want anything to drink?"* he asks. *"I'm parched."*

"Yeah," I say. *"Parched."*

But this is all, of course, just in my imagination.

I open the fridge and look in. I see brown eggs in a dish, organic yogurt, organic chocolate milk, almond milk, some organic smoothie-looking drinks, a casserole that must have been taken out of the freezer to thaw, some chicken breasts from chickens raised cage-free, some ready-made salads and salad dressings. I think about how expensive all that fancy food must be. In one drawer is a block of Toll House cookie dough. I think about how good cookies would be right now, maybe with some of that almond milk.

"You like almond milk?" he asks, lifting the carton.

"Mm-hmm." I nod. He pours two glasses, both to the brim, and turns—*"Whoops"*—sloshing some of the milk down the front of his shirt. *"Oh, well. You know my motto. No shirt, no problem, am I right?"*

I want to stop thinking about this.

I mean, it's not like I haven't seen Matt naked before. I've seen him undress in the locker room loads of times, but that's different, way different, in fact. Being alone with him in a room—*his* room, no less—watching him slide out of his clothes so casually, just talking to me, as if this is part of our routine and shortly we'll be brushing our teeth together, turning out the lights, and crawling into bed.

Truth: I'm still hard at this point. In fact, I'm starting to think not even the near-frozen cookie dough can hold a candle to me. I'm about to bite off a square of the dough when I spot the door to what has to be a bathroom around the corner. I step over to it, move inside, and swing the door softly shut behind me.

I find the light switch and flip it. It's not a bathroom, it turns out, but a laundry room. There's a washing machine and a dryer stacked one on top of the other—I've never seen a washer and dryer like this before. Pretty decent way to save space, if you ask me. There's also a short little ironing board with some bright collared shirts draped over it. I kneel beside the ironing board. "Okay," I say. I unbutton, unzip, and pull at the waist of my jeans.

"Okay," I say again. I shut my eyes. Remember.

I start going to town with myself behind the closed door of Matt's laundry room, in Matt's house. At first it feels all weird and kind of exciting, but then it becomes just like every other time I've done this, and I lose track of everything. It's like I go elsewhere. There's a pounding in my chest. A pounding throughout my body. A pounding on the door.

A pounding on the door?

My eyes shoot open.

"Tretch?" It's Matt on the other side. "You in there?"

My brain floods. *No! No! No! No!*

I keep quiet. Then the door starts to open.

"Uh! Wait, wait!" I holler. *What now?* "Hold on just a second, Matt!"

"Tretch, why are you in the laundry room?"

I stand up fast and jump over by the washing machine, staring into it. "Just checking the appliances!" I try to sound calm. My pants are still around my knees. I yank them up. "You can come in," I say.

Matt pushes the door open. "Ah," he says. "You like the washing machine?"

"I really do!" I say. I make sure to keep my front turned away from him. "It's nice, the way they're stacked."

"Did you want some cookies? I saw you had the dough pulled out."

"Oh! Yeah. I would love some—" I clear my throat. "Cookies."

"Sweet," Matt says. "Me, too." He disappears out of the doorway, and I adjust myself, zipping up my pants and all. *Does he really not know?* I'm not sure. He doesn't seem to be acting weird, at least.

When I get out of the laundry room, Matt is standing by the oven, breaking apart squares of cookie dough and putting them on a rectangular metal baking sheet. He is shirtless, wearing some long green pajama pants.

It's almost like in my fantasy—except that it's not. "Shower's free, if you want it," he says. "I left some pajamas out for you."

"Thanks—I think I just might," I tell him. "Be right back." I bound up the stairs.

Once my clothes are off, I turn the shower knob to cold and stand under the freezing stream. I'm still anxious.

He doesn't know, I think. *He doesn't know.*

He came close, but he doesn't know.

Later, Matt and I, still with damp hair and smelling like Old Spice body wash, sit on his bed watching an episode of *The Office* on Landon's laptop. "I don't know where I'd be if you hadn't told me about this show," he says.

I shrug. "One day you'll find a way to repay me."

We fall asleep side by side with the laptop sitting on the edge of the bed. At one point in the night, I wake up and see it teetering. I sit up, reach across Matt, and set it gently on the floor. My arm over his bare chest—I can't help it. I think about kissing him. Like it's the most normal thing on earth.

I'm imagining us being like his dads. Living in a house that's ours, sleeping in a bed we share, and not caring what anybody thinks about it. Just being in love.

I wake up to Matt's face hovering over me, smiling. *"Riiise and shiiiiiine,"* he says.

I cover my eyes. "*Ugghh*, morning," I groan.

"Come on. Dad and Pop are making breakfast."

We stumble downstairs to the scent of brewing coffee and frying bacon. The sounds are of sizzling and popping, and a dull gurgle. Ron stands at the frying pan, humming, his short hair in sprouts around the tops of his ears. Landon, ponytailed and bearded, with his square-rimmed glasses, sets plates on the kitchen table.

"Hey, hey, guys," he says.

Ron turns around. "Morning, boys."

"Morning."

"Morning."

I eye the laundry room guiltily.

"Matthew." Ron points the fork he was using to turn the bacon at his son. "We heard you come in last night. Cutting it awful close to midnight, weren't you?"

Matt hangs his head. "Yes," he says. "But we had to walk Amy home."

"Mm-hmmmm. 'Had to'?" Ron winks at me. "Hear that, Landon?"

"Heard it." Landon looks up from his place setting and smiles. "So, Tretch, can you confirm or deny whether Matt's got a thing for this Amy Sinks?"

I shoot a glance at Matt, and he rolls his eyes.

"Confirmed it!" Ron says. "We knew it." He reaches for a high five from Landon, who slaps him one.

"I figured we'd know a crush from our boy when we saw one." Landon pulls some napkins from a cabinet. "Sure enough"—he winks at Matt—"we did."

"Come *on*, guys! Leave it alone, please."

Ron smirks and turns the bacon in the pan. "Whatever," he says. "Tretch, you drink OJ or just coffee?"

"Hmm."

"Too long to decide," Landon says. "He gets both." He hands me and Matt a mug each. The one I get has a snowman on it, with the word *BUM* in uppercase underneath it. I don't get it. I nudge Matt to look at it, but he just shrugs. He tips hot coffee from the pot into our mugs and we sit down. Landon delivers a cup of orange juice to my place, and I can't help but think it's the nicest thing. He sits down and unfolds a paper. Ron puts a plate of hot bacon in front of us, layered with paper towels. "It's turkey bacon," he says. "Hope you don't mind, Tretch."

"Oh, I *love* turkey bacon, Mr. Ron," I say, even though I've never had it. But, as it turns out, I really do love it. After my first piece, I scarf down three more. We all sit chewing and sipping in silence for a while. It's nice, the sunlight coming in through the kitchen windows, which are still drawn with thin curtains, and spreading itself out along the table. The oven dings and Ron gets up, returning with a pan of hot biscuits. He drops one onto his plate, one onto Landon's, and two onto Matt's plate and mine.

"Thanks, Pop," Matt says.

"Thanks, Mr. Ron," I say.

"You're welcome, you're welcome." Ron sits down, smiling. "Now, Matt, your dad and I want to *know* about this girl. I mean, what's she like? You can't just keep us in the dark about—"

"*Pop!*" Matt's eyes go big. "I will talk about it when there is something to talk about." Matt looks at me, and I stop chewing. "I promise. But, honestly, there's nothing to talk about at the moment, right, Tretch?"

I swallow. "Well . . ."

"Aha!" Ron leans in.

"Okay, so there *is* something!" Landon says. "Tretch *clearly* thinks so."

"Tretch is on our side!" Ron proclaims. "I *knew* I liked this kid." He looks at Landon and gestures to me with his thumb. All of this is in good fun, of course. I know they're just acting this way to give Matt a hard time. It's a kind of messing around, a kind of friendly talk, and it supplies the kitchen with a warmth separate from that of the coffee or the frying pan.

Matt turns to Ron. "*Dad.*" Then he turns to Landon. "*Pop.* I don't want to talk about it. Yes, I kind of have a crush on this girl, and, yes, I think she might like me, too, but . . ." He spreads his hands wide. "I don't want to talk about it before anything is certain, okay? Like, I don't want to jinx it."

"Well, what are you waiting for to happen, Matt?"

"Yeah, I'm confused."

Matt's dads each take sips from the same coffee mug, one that reads MONDAY and has a picture of a cartoonish, red-eyed squirrel on it.

Matt smacks his forehead with his hand. "Well, I'm not talking about *sex*, if that's what you guys are thinking."

"Well, you kind of made it sound like—"

"You *did* make it sound—"

Matt eyes me. I shrug again. I realize this is one breakfast table where sometimes even keeping your mouth shut gets you into trouble.

"Tretch, back me up here."

I clear my throat, which feels almost chapped from the orange juice and coffee. "Um . . . I think Matt doesn't want it to get out, you know? Like, he doesn't want to act like it's official until it actually is official."

"Understandable," Landon concedes.

Matt pats me on the back. "True friend," he says.

"That *is* a true friend," Ron says.

"True friend, indeed," Landon agrees through a biscuit-filled mouth.

"You guys are acting weird," Matt says. "Are you all amped about the trip or something?"

"Of course!" Ron says. Then he looks over at Landon and hands him a napkin. "You got crumbs in your beard."

"Oh, whoops." Landon flicks his beard a couple times

with his finger. The crumbs stay. "Yeah, we're pretty *amped*, I guess." He giggles. "Are you, Matt?"

"Yeah."

"When are y'all leaving?" I ask.

"Tomorrow."

"Tomorrow?" I'm surprised. I haven't wanted to think about them leaving, but here it is. Can't we all just stay here for the entire rest of break?

Ron, with another napkin, wipes a spot of grease from the table. "Yeah. Matt, you gotta make sure you're all packed tonight."

"I know," Matt says. He looks at me and rolls his eyes again. "We're leaving in the morning."

"Dang," I say, which isn't an eighth of what I'm feeling. "I guess I didn't realize it was so soon."

"You're gonna be bored slap to death, aren't you?"

I can't look him in the eye right now. It's too difficult, because I'm too afraid of what he might see.

"I know," I tell the table. "Without you or Joe around, I don't know what I'm gonna—"

"Movies," Landon suggests. He looks at me and smiles. "Watch lots and *lots* of movies."

There's no way for me to tell him that this is the movie I want to watch, this is the one I want to be in, this scene right here.

ten

With both Joe and Matt gone, I am *so bored*.

I spend a lot of time wondering, mostly about my future.

I wonder if it would be a good idea to run away. Or maybe I'll just wait until I'm eighteen, make good grades, get into an out-of-state school, make even better grades, and then move to LA to write and direct a sitcom or something.

Maybe a sitcom about my life. About a kid growing up in a small town, figuring out he's got a crush on his best guy friend, figuring it out while he's *in church*, no less. I wonder if that would even make it on TV. Wonder if anyone would want to know about a story like that. It would be sad but not any more than it had to be. I mean, my life isn't sad. My life is good, with some sad, hard things scattered around it.

The thing is, on a TV show there always has to be something happening. And right now, with Matt and Joe gone, nothing is.

When I can't bear it anymore, I go and hang out with Spooky the Bad Luck Cat, since I think we're trying to make amends. The day after Matt leaves, I go across the street to the Whips' house and sit with her, rubbing her black hair. She actually purrs when I do this, which is nice. Then I have to open that nasty, wet Fancy Feast to feed her, and I just about hurl.

When I walk out the Whips' front door, I notice something funny. Dad's car is there in the middle of the day. I wonder if he's come home for lunch. I know Mom's home, so maybe he's decided to eat with us.

The sky is white and makes the day feel snowed in, even though it never snows in Warmouth. I keep my hands in my pockets and arms against my sides as I walk up the front lawn to the house.

When I walk in, I see a loaf of bread on the countertop.

"Hey, Dad?" I call.

I walk down the hallway to Mom and Dad's bedroom. The door is shut.

What does that *mean? Surely Mom and Dad aren't—*

"Ugh," I say, starting to turn.

But then I hear Dad's voice. And I stop.

Because there's something about the way he sounds. He's talking really fast, almost like he's speaking gibberish. I stand in the hallway, wondering. And then I wonder if it would be okay to listen, just eavesdrop a little. I mean, if something's wrong, I want to know about it.

I creep up to the door and press my ear against it.

"—I don't know, Katy, he left a voice mail. That was all."

"Well, did you try calling back? Maybe that would—"

"I tried, but they aren't answering."

Dad sighs—and not the quiet kind of sigh, either. It's a worried sigh, like the kind you use when you can't really say what you're trying to say, and you feel all this pressure or something stopping up the inside of your chest. It comes out of him like a low roar.

"Where's Tretch?" he asks.

"He's feeding Spooky."

"Oh, okay."

"We shouldn't—"

"No, we shouldn't say anything."

Suddenly, I feel dizzy.

In the fifth grade, Mom gave me this talk about "adult things." She had just walked in on me reading this old book of hers called *The Thorn Birds*, and she wasn't very happy about it.

"There are adult things, Tretch, and there are kid things," she had explained. "When you're older, this book will be fine."

Right now, I know I'm on the outside of an adult thing, looking in. And I'm not sure I want to be.

I stop listening and walk down the hallway to the living room, where I slide beneath the Christmas tree. They will notice me here; they will notice me, and then maybe they will figure I've heard them. Then maybe they'll tell me about it, if they think I can handle it—whatever *it* is.

Right above my nose is this ornament I got from the Samsanuk Opera House, right after I saw *The Nutcracker* with Mom. It's a blond Clara in ballet slippers holding her nutcracker. I blow softly and watch it shake. There's something about it that soothes me.

I close my eyes and fall asleep, and I dream about the Christmas tree. I dream that it grows bigger and bigger, like the tree in *The Nutcracker*, and I can hear all this chirping coming from beneath it. I don't know what it is, either, until I start to float up. When I look down, I see what's causing all the chirping.

Rats.

Just like in *The Nutcracker*. Like the Mouse King and all his cronies. They're scuffling around all over the presents and stuff—

"*Bagh!*" I wake up shouting. My head shoots up into the tree's bottom branches, and I get a mouthful of pine needles. Two glass ornaments shake free of their stems. They crash and break on the floor.

"Oh no!" I cry out, childlike. I hop up, run into the kitchen, and grab a broom and a dustpan. One of the ornaments is pretty plain-looking, just kind of a red ball, no big loss, but the other one upsets me. I can still read the letters on the broken glass.

Our Family

It's an old ornament with all of us drawn as stick figures on it: Dad as the tallest stick figure with pants, Mom the stick figure with a dress, Joe smaller, and me the smallest. I can't just throw it away, even if it is broken.

I carry the dustpan upstairs to my bedroom, take Grandma's scarf out of my desk drawer, and put the ornament shards there instead.

Then I sit down on the bed and start to cry.

I can't explain it. It's not just the broken feeling. It's being responsible as well. But even that isn't enough for why I feel so emotional right now. Maybe I'm getting sick.

In, like, third grade, Grandma had to take me to the doctor's office because I was sick with something. I don't even remember what it was. I just remember feeling awful, and I was crying, and I mean *crying*, really sobbing, and Grandma was sitting with me in the waiting room with her arm around me, rubbing my shoulder.

I remember dripping snot on the front of my T-shirt and snorting the question, "Grandma, do you think I'm brave?"

She just nodded and held a hanky up to my nose. "Yes, I think you are very brave, Tretch," she said. "Now, blow." I didn't think it was possible for me to be brave and be crying at the same time.

Truth: I always get kind of emotional when I get sick. It always makes me feel like a big wimp, too.

I stand up and go to the stereo, where a CD Joe burned for me before he left is sitting, ready to be played. He remembered to put that Ellie Goulding song I like so much on it—and, over the past day or two, I've been developing a new dance to it in my room. I decide to dance now to take my mind off things for a little while. Maybe I'll feel better afterward.

The trouble with dancing to this song is the *eeh-eeh-eeh* parts at the very beginning, because I want what I do during those *eeh-eeh-eeh*s to be different than what I do during the *eeh-eeh-eeh*s that come later.

So I've been trying some stuff.

It's really hard to cry and sweat at the same time, so the dancing does the trick. After a few go-rounds, I've sweated a whole lot. My face is all moist and pink when I check it in the mirror. I decide to take what I call a *Dirty Dancing* break. This is when I go downstairs to the living room and stick my DVD of *Dirty Dancing* into the player. I've had about four *Dirty Dancing* breaks in the last couple of days.

"Tretch, *Dirty Dancing* again?" Mom asks when she walks into the living room.

If I were feeling better, I might ask her about the discussion I overheard. I might ask her if everything's okay with Dad. She's already told me that work has been tough for him lately, I know, but he sounded—well, he sounded *upset*. I've heard him sound *worried* about stuff going on at Farm and Handel before, but never *upset*.

Now that I'm not dancing, my body's acting all weird on its own.

"Mom, I don't feel too well," I say. "I think I'm getting sick."

"Uh-oh," she says. "What you think you got, Tretch-o?" She comes over and feels my head. "We'll have to get your dad to check. He's better at telling fevers than me. *Richard*—"

"Yep?"

Dad comes in, and I turn off *Dirty Dancing*. Mom drapes this quilt that Grandma made me from all these different pieces of fabric, all different colors, shapes, and designs, over my legs. Then she goes and slides the Dolly Parton and Kenny Rogers Christmas CD into the stereo to cheer me up.

"Okay, Tretch-o." Dad presses his hand against my forehead. Then, like he isn't getting a good enough read on it, he turns his head and pushes his cheek up against my face.

"Yep," he says. "It's a fever."

It could also be dancing, but I don't tell him that.

Mom puts her hand on her hip. "Better take it easy, then, Tretch. Here, I'll bring you some Tylenol."

"All right," I tell her. There's always something about knowing you're sick that makes you feel sicker. So I slump over onto the couch and bang my head against the solid armrest. "Ow," I say, but I say it kind of sarcastically, because I know it was probably pretty funny to watch. I look up at Dad, but he isn't laughing. He's scratching absently at some stubble on his chin. "Dad, you're getting some scruff," I comment.

"Oh . . . yeah," he says, sounding a little embarrassed that I noticed. "It's time I switch out my razor blade I guess."

"No, I like it! It reminds me of Matt's dad, Mr. Landon. He's got a big old scruffy beard."

"Yeah, that man looks like a hippie." Dad touches his chin another moment. "I couldn't pull it off, I don't think." He smiles at me. "You want me to make you some soup, Tretch?"

"Nah, I'm good."

"Starve a cold, feed a fever. That's how it goes."

"It's the other way around, Richard!" Mom calls from the kitchen. "*Starve* a fever, feed a cold."

Dad looks at me and shrugs. "Whoops."

Mom emerges with two Tylenols in hand. "Okay, I want you to swallow these, then I want you to go get some rest." She hands me some cold water in a mug. I take the Tylenol and sip the water. Then I stand and walk up the stairs, each step feeling heavier than the last. "I feel *weeeeaaaak*," I complain. "I *haaaate* sickness."

I put my hands on the step above me and drag my feet along, eventually ending in a heap on the carpet at the top of the stairs.

"Tretch, no drama," Mom says from the bottom of the stairs. "Go get in the bed."

"*Ugggghhhh.*" I crawl along the hall to my bed, crawl up into it, and lie there, blaming Joe and Matt for leaving me alone during the holidays. As if the loneliness is what got me sick.

It's a drag. But eventually I do fall asleep.

When I wake up later, I'm shivering and wet with sweat.

"Freezing, f-freezing," I stutter, rolling out from under my covers.

The Night of the Winter Fever.

I step, all sticky-feeling, down the hall to the bathroom, thinking a shower will be good. *What time is it?* I wonder. In the bathroom, I take off all my damp clothes. My T-shirt feels slimy coming up over my head. I slide off my pajama pants and underwear, turn the shower handle, and sit naked on the toilet, watching the steam fog up the mirror. I'm not exactly sure how much time has passed by the time I step past the curtain and stand under the hot water. I shiver at first, but it feels nice, standing there. Every time I feel like I'm getting used to the heat, I turn it up a little more. I keep it nice and hot. Eventually, I sit down, which I've never done in the shower before, but that makes my knees cold, so I decide to get out. I wobble up onto my feet again, reach for the handle, and make an effort to turn it. I notice I'm seeing everything like a TV screen, and the edges are fading, like a movie that's about to end, King Kong, bullet-riddled, dropping from the sky, and I'm dropping, too, except for its more like kneeling but fast. *"Dad—"* I say. The shower drain rises toward my face.

I pass out.

But only for, like, a second, I'm pretty sure.

"Daaaad!" I call. "Dad, I'm pretty sure I just fainted!"

I stagger to my feet and turn off the water. Then I wrap a towel around me. In a second, Dad is at the door. "Tretch?"

"Hey, Dad."

"Did you just faint?"

"Yes, but it was very fast." The whole bathroom feels like it's on a tilt. My hip bangs the edge of the sink, and I'm scared my towel will fall.

"Here, Tretch." Dad slings his arm around me. "Lean on me."

"Richard?" Mom calls from the bottom of the stairs. "Is everything okay?"

"Tretch is fine," Dad says. "A little dehydrated. Fix him some water, will you, Katy?"

Dad walks me to my room, where I sit down on the edge of the bed. Mom brings me a cup of cold water. I drink the whole thing.

"Phew," I say after I've downed it.

"Feel better?" Mom asks.

"Yes," I say.

"Stay there. I want you to drink a bit more." Dad takes the cup down to the kitchen and fills it up again.

They make me drink two more cups. Then make sure I'm okay in bed.

And what I feel through my feverish haze is gratitude. In moments like this, I can believe their care for me is unconditional. In moments like this, I almost forget to be afraid.

eleven

The next day I wake up and immediately breathe a sigh of relief. I feel bizarrely (but wonderfully) better. I can tell my fever has broken. I know that Christmas Eve is tomorrow. I know that Joe will be home in the morning.

The ride to Farm Farm is only a day away.

But, for the time being, I need to get out of my sickbed. I decide to go to Mabel's and see if Amy is working. Maybe she's gotten a report from Matt in New York. I wonder if he, Landon, and Ron have already gone to see *Hedwig and the Angry Inch* or not.

I pull on my corduroy pants, which are a little too big around my waist, and cinch them tight with the "vegan" belt Mom got me for my birthday. I think it looks nice, so I decide to also wear a good shirt, a light blue one, kind of icy-looking, and a dark blue jacket. Looking at all the blue, I remember Mr. Thumb's scarf. I reach into the top drawer of my dresser, pull it out, and wrap it around my neck.

"Daaaaang, Tretch," I say, looking it over in the mirror.

I hop down the steps at a pretty quick clip, and Mom sticks her head through the kitchen doorway.

"Feelin' better, Tretch-o?" she asks.

"Yes, ma'am."

"Good. I was hoping it'd only be a twenty-four hour thing."

"Yeah, me, too." I look at the clock on the kitchen stove. It's nearly noon. "I think I want to go downtown and grab some hot chocolate. Be nice to see Amy."

"She's a cutie pie."

I sigh. "Yeah."

Mom disappears into the kitchen. I hear a whisk going, and I know she's already preparing for the Farm Farm Christmas Feast Marathon. Whatever she's working on, it smells awesome.

"Well, have fun!" she calls. "But don't be gone long. You're still on the mend, you know."

"I won't be long!" I call, already out the back door. I take my secret passage to Barrow Street through the Yarborough Antiques parking lot. The scarf flaps in the wind against my shoulder. I feel a little hop in my step that I haven't felt during the past couple days. It feels good to be out.

Barrow Street is more crowded than ever, with people going into stores. I walk by Books and look in the window. There's a line that wraps entirely around the young adult section, so I guess the sale must be doing them good. I don't see Lana at the counter—instead, there's just this tall, skinny dude with black hair. I assume it's her cousin, the one who owns the place. The door to Jim Cho's swings open and a mom with two boys ambles out. Both boys look flushed with pleasure after their talks with Santa, and the mom looks pretty happy, too. Seeing them makes me think about when Joe and I would go see Santa when we were little. Good memories, except for one time when I smacked Santa in the chin on accident and popped his beard off, and another time when Joe threw up. He doesn't let me tell that story to everyone, but when we talk about it, just the two of us, he says, *"I was so excited, I threw up!"* And it is really, extremely funny.

Things are calm at Mabel's. I walk in and seat myself. Quiet piano music plays over the stereo system, and I don't see Amy. I actually don't see anyone working except for Mabel herself, standing by the baked goods display, talking to a middle-aged woman in a parka. Mabel is talking up a slice of berry-filled coffee cake. "It's an all-natural *organic* cake," she says, "made by one of our waitresses." I wonder if she's talking about Amy. I wouldn't be surprised to find out that Amy is, in addition to being beautiful and a talented dancer, an excellent baker.

Because, you know, that's fair.

Just then, the door to the kitchen opens, and out walks a waitress. Not Amy Sinks, though, walking with her proud, upbeat, hip-shaking strut.

No, instead it's Lana Kramer, wearing the bright pink Mabel's apron and holding another platter of coffee cake covered in Saran Wrap.

"There she is!" Mabel says. "There's our baker girl!"

Lana walks the coffee cake over to a married couple sitting in a booth sipping coffee. "Here you go," she says. "It's twelve bucks. I'll just put it on your ticket." She looks up and catches sight of me. This flusters her.

I slide down into my booth. *Should've brought a book*, I think, and then, *Wait, no, because then Lana would want to talk about it with me.* I reach for a copy of *The Mouth* that's sitting in a chair a table over from me. I hold it up, trying to hide myself. That's when I see the cover story:

TEEN SUICIDE IN SAMSANUK:
BULLYING OVER SEXUAL ORIENTATION
CAUSES DEATH

I feel an itch in my throat and cough. *Yesterday morning, 15-year-old . . .* the article begins. I move my hand to cover up the boy's picture. Too late. I've seen it. The class-photo smile. I haven't read his name, though. I don't want to know. I'm scared to. I—

"Pretty sad, huh?" Lana stands over me. Her dark hair is tied up in a ponytail. She has on the same pink glasses as when I saw her working the register at Books the other day. She's holding a notepad to take orders.

I gulp. "Yeah."

"Hang on just a second. I've gotta run this check to them." She skips over to a table, hands the people there a check.

When she returns, she sits down like I've invited her to join me. "Can I get you anything?" she asks.

I felt bad saying yes now that she's sat down. Because isn't that the same as asking her to get back up?

"Uhh . . ." I start.

"Hot chocolate?"

I shrug. "A hot chocolate would be great."

Lana takes off her glasses. "Okay, now let me just get the attention of one of the waitresses around here." She mock waves her hand in the air, then, looking down at her apron, jokes, "Oh, what do you know?"

I fudge a grin.

"Just kidding," she says, putting her glasses back on. Then she stands up and walks across the restaurant, and in a quick span of time is back seated at the table with two cups of hot chocolate. "It's time for my break, anyways," she tells me. She holds her own steaming cup to her mouth and sips. "Mmm," she says. I take a sip myself and don't say anything. I also make a point to look down at my hands and avoid eye contact. If Lana thinks I'm being awkward, well, good. Maybe she'll stop liking me.

"So how are those books treating you, Tretch?" she asks.

I look up. "What books?"

Lana leans back against her chair. "The ones you got at the store the other day, remember? *On the Road*, right? And *A Separate Peace*?"

"Oh yeah," I say. Then I mumble guiltily, "Honestly, I haven't even started them yet, Lana. I've been kind of sick lately."

"Oof. That sucks."

"When did you get a job at Mabel's?"

"Well. Long story short, my cousin fired me from Books."

"What? *Why?*" I'm shocked, and the force of my reaction makes Lana smile.

"I might have just *borrowed* a little too much merchandise without paying for it." She turns her head to the side and uses her shoulder to rub her chin. "I always planned to give everything back, though. Or pay for it eventually. But it slipped my mind."

I think about that. I want to say, *But the book you gave me you paid for.* I saw her pay for it. She'd even covered the penny for me.

"Hmm, how much merchandise?" I have to ask.

"My cousin said there were close to fifty books unaccounted for in our inventory."

"Oh my *gosh*, Lana. Are you going to return them?"

"Like I said, I plan to *eventually*." Lana grins. "So, Tretch, has Amy Sinks, uh—has Amy Sinks mentioned anything to you about her New Year's dance?"

Oh no, I think. *Here it comes.* I cough in a panic, hot chocolate burning the inside of my throat. It doesn't matter if she thinks I like her or not. She's going to ask me anyway.

"Uhhh . . . what?" I stare stupidly.

Lana looks at me with wide eyes, both her eyebrows arched. "Uh, well," she says, "Tretch, I wanted to ask you—"

We're interrupted by the sound of chairs scraping as the couple sitting across from us stands. Lana's eyes dart. "Oops," she says. "Hold that thought. I'll be right back."

She gets up.

"Lana, wait," I say.

She waits. And I can tell from her expression that she's waiting for good news. Or at least hoping for it.

"I'm actually gonna have to take this to go," I say. "I just remembered—I was supposed to meet my mom, like, five minutes ago." I pull out my wallet and set down a five-dollar bill. "I'm really sorry to bail so fast."

I scoot out of my seat.

"Oh," she says. "But, Tretch, I was gonna—"

I freeze. Even though I'm dreading what's coming next, I know I can't just dash. Not while she's midsentence.

"I was gonna—" She swallows. Pauses. Looks at me. "Oh, never mind. I'll see ya around."

"Yeah, see ya, Lana."

I'm out the door before she can change her mind.

twelve

I figure I'm off the hook. But that night, Lana calls our house. Mom answers, and when she yells up, "Tretch! Phone's for you!" I'm overjoyed.

I'm overjoyed because I'm convinced that, finally, it's Matt. But when I look at her and mouth, *Matt?* as she hands over the phone, she shakes her head.

"Hello?" I ask into the receiver.

"Tretch?"

"Oh, uh—"

"*Hi!* It's Lana Kramer."

"Oh, uh, hey, Lana."

"*Hey.* So I didn't get to finish talking to you today, but"—I shut my eyes and grit my teeth—"you know how we were talking about Amy Sinks's dance party?"

"Yeah." I sigh, aiming away from the mouthpiece.

"Okay, well, do you want to go with me? I mean, I didn't even realize it was going to be a date thing, you know, but apparently people are—"

"Okay," I say. Because I can't figure out a way not to.

"Apparently people are asking, which I thought was weird, and you know I don't really do the whole—"

"Okay."

"Huh? What'd you say, Tretch?"

I press the phone against my temple. "I said *okay*, Lana. I'll be your date."

"Blech! Isn't *date* just the weirdest word?"

I want to beat my head against the wall. "Yes, it is kind of weird."

"But, *alas*, what other word is there for it?"

"Beats me."

"Ahhh! Tretch, I am so excited!"

"Me, too, Lana," I say, and then something happens: a click.

Did she just hang up?

"Tretch? Are you there?"

"Yeah!" I say. Then I tone it down. "Yeah, I'm here. I thought you'd hung up, Lana."

"Yeah. I thought you had, too—" Then she interrupts herself. "Oh, *God*." I'm pretty sure I hear her facepalm. "I think that was my *mom*."

I snort. "What?"

"Ugghh. My *mom*, Tretch. She's been psycho about this whole thing—"

"What whole thing?"

"This whole date business. My *God*."

"Why's she being psycho?"

"She just, *ugh*. Never mind. I won't go into it." Now it's Lana's turn to sigh. "She just wants me to—"

I'm quiet. I don't know if she wants me to ask, or what.

"—never mind."

"Okay, Lana." I let it drop.

"Well, I really am looking so forward to the dance! Thank you so much!"

There's something sad about this. The fact that she feels like she has to thank me. "Oh, uh, thank *you*, Lana," I say.

"Well, I'll see you, Tretch."

"Oh, okay. Bye."

Her end clicks; then there's the dial tone. I'm going to need time to process everything that just happened. I hook the phone back to the receiver and walk into the living room, where Mom and Dad are seated on the couch.

The TV isn't on, nothing. It's a setup, and I know it.

"Who was that, Tretch-o?" Mom asks. I can tell by her smile that she has an idea.

"Oh," I say, stopping at the base of the stairs, "it was just Lana."

Dad scratches his chin. "Is that the girl you can't stand who works at the bookshop?"

With that, Mom smacks Dad on the thigh with her palm. "No, silly!" she says. "I mean, yes, that's who you're thinking of. But this is the girl Tretch went on a *date* with the other night."

"A double date," I correct, lest Mom's excitement run away with her. I slip my hands into my pockets. "But, yeah, I mean, she's pretty cool." I find a piece of lint and pinch. "She, uh, she just asked me to Amy Sinks's New Year's dance—"

Mom jolts up. "Oh, Tretch, that's *wonderful.*" She knocks the remote control onto the floor. "That's, uh—" She bends down to pick it up. "That's *exciting*, don't you think?"

"Yeah," I say, doing my best to sound excited. "It is, uh, very exciting." Somehow it falls flat. I don't want them to be excited about this, because it makes me even more worried about the truth, which is the opposite of this.

Dad gives me a thumbs-up fist pump, a classic sign of approval. "Way to go, Tretch," he says.

"Yeah, well—"

He grins. "Getting to be a regular old ladies' man, aren't you?"

No, I think. *Stop. You don't know what you're doing.*

"Oh, uh—" I shake my head. "I don't know." I turn away from them and start up the stairs.

"Just let us know the details when you find out!" Mom calls. "I'd be happy to drive y'all!"

I holler back, "Thanks, Mom!"

I shut the door to my room and throw myself down on my bed. *Don't worry about it, don't worry about it, don't worry about it*, I think, and then, finally, *Parents are so weird.*

I pull a pillow over the top of my head and breathe.

The next morning, Joe returns, and Mom and Dad kick into full-on Christmas Eve Frenzy mode.

"Tretch, I need you to carry Grandma and Granddad's presents to the car—will you do that for me?" Mom is wearing a blue sweatshirt with a snowman on it and present-shaped earrings. "*Oh*, and if you could get those two casseroles from the fridge, I'd really appreciate it."

Dad wears his hunting jacket but keeps the collar cinched tight around his neck to hide the rash. "Tretch, are you not dressed yet, son? What's the holdup?"

Joe sits at the table, all droopy-eyed from his early flight, his hands wrapped around a cup of coffee.

"Hey, Joe," I say.

"Hey, Tretch."

"You tired?"

"Yeah."

"How was Dallas?"

"Dallas was okay," he says, his head nodding sleepily. "You got a present. Here. Since it's not under the tree, I think you're allowed to open it now."

It's a small rectangular present, wrapped in bright red paper and sprinkled with a couple dead tree needles. Nana and Papa always give the coolest gifts, usually stuff they picked up while traveling abroad.

I rip the paper, tossing it ferociously to the side.

What? Why the—?

It's a copy of *Chitty Chitty Bang Bang.*

"Real thoughtful," I mumble. "Yet inarguably disappointing."

"What is it?" Joe asks, his face in his hand. He looks so sleepy I think he might tip out of his chair.

"A *Chitty Chitty Bang Bang* DVD?"

"Aw, you used to love that movie."

"Are you kidding? It used to scare me. That freakin' childnapper? And how old do they think I am, anyway?"

Dad walks in and pulls the casseroles from the fridge—which Mom asked me to do. He looks annoyed, and he's starting to sound it. "Better get movin', Tretch-o. We gotta go." He crosses the kitchen to the open front door.

"Be ready in two seconds," I say.

I turn and rush back up the stairs to brush my teeth and change into some jeans. To be honest, it ends up taking me more like *fifty* seconds before I'm ready. Still, that's pretty fast, I think.

In the driveway, I pile into the back of the Accord next to Joe. And then I remember, "*Oh*, my CD player!"

"Come on," Dad says. "You don't need—"

But I'm already up and out of the seat, scurrying back to the house.

"Tretch, the door is *locked*," Mom calls out the window. I spin around and stare at her. *I need my CD player.* Dad turns off the car and pulls the key out. Mom tosses them to me through the passenger window.

I'm on a roll this morning. I know I'm on their nerves. But it's okay. They know I'll go crazy if I have to ride out to Farm Farm with no music.

The CD player is on the kitchen counter where I set it the night before. I snag it, run, and lock the door in record time.

"All *right*," I say, reseating myself next to Joe. He's already nodding off against the window. His head pops up when Dad cranks the ignition, then droops back down again. I put my headphones on and hit play.

"*Eeh, eeh, eeh, eeh-eeh, eeh . . .*"

I lose track of how many times I play the song over the course of the ride. Once, I press pause to ask Mom a question:

"If I want to send Matt a Christmas card, how long would it take to get to New York?"

Mom is in the middle of saying something to Dad, but she stops and turns to answer me. "It's already Christmas Eve, Tretch. It's much too late for that."

I nod. But I don't really care all that much if it actually gets to Matt by Christmas. I kind of just care that it gets to him at all. So he'll know I'm thinking about him—without him knowing I'm thinking about him *too* much.

I have just hit play again on the CD player when Mom says something else. I pause it again.

"Huh?" I say. But then I realize she isn't speaking to me.

"Richard, it might not even be that bad. We'll just have to see."

Dad nods. "So why keep it a secret, then?"

I gulp. *What are they talking about?* I glance at Joe. *Surely Joe hasn't told them about—*

"I left another message on their machine," Dad says. "But they're not calling back."

I feel a little tension release from my chest. It can't be me, then, that they're talking about. But then who is it?

I start to daydream about Mom and Dad being a part of some secret group of spies—a kind of underground special agency. Or like X-Men, mutants. And Joe and I are mutants, too.

We just haven't discovered our powers yet.

. .

We park under the old pine tree next to the driveway, and I don't skip a beat. I fly from the car, through the garage where Granddad's old Ford is parked, and through the front door. The smell of coffee hits me, and I stomp my feet on the holiday welcome mat, the same old holiday welcome mat that Grandma puts out every year: 'TIS THE SEASON.

I take off my tennis shoes and fling them into the pantry beside the entrance. Then, in my socks, I skid into the kitchen.

Grandma is at the kitchen table, shuffling a deck of cards. A steaming cup of coffee sits to the right of her quick hands, and her wig sits sort of lopsided on top of her head.

"Well, hellooo," I say, crossing from carpet to tile into the kitchen. I speak everything like it comes with a drum roll: a symptom of my excitement. "Grandmaaa, whatcha doiiing?"

Her head snaps up, and the wig slides back a little farther from her forehead. Her eyes are wide, like I've startled her.

"Well, look who it is!" she exclaims.

"Merry Christmas!" I say, wrapping my arms around her shoulders, whiffing the old-closet smell of the bright red sweatshirt she wears and, beneath it, the smell of the Irish Spring bath soap she and Granddad always use. She hugs me in a Farm Farm bear hug, her cheek pressed against mine, feeling wrinkled and soft.

"How's it going?" I ask.

"Going good." She nods, her wig sliding forward ever so slightly. "Same old, pretty much." She squeezes both of my hands, our customary greeting.

Mom, Dad, and Joe filter into the kitchen, lugging casseroles and presents. I figure Dad'll probably say something right about now, about me not helping ("Way to lend a hand, Tretch" or something—kind of joking but also kind of not), but he doesn't. He sets the package he's carrying down, crosses directly over to Grandma, and pulls her close. "Hey, Mom," he says.

"Well, hello, hello, Richard," she replies.

"Where's Dad?"

"He's out back, tending to the fire."

Mom places a hand on my arm. "Hey, babe, will you run out to the car and get the last two casseroles? Joe, I guess you had better go take a nap—"

Joe yawns. "Hey, Grandma. What's up?"

"Get over here and give me a hug." Grandma gives Joe a stern once-over. "You take an early flight, young man?" She reaches out her hands, and Joe places his on top.

"Yes, ma'am," he says.

"Well, you better get rested up, then. We got too much food to eat to not have you around."

Joe smiles at that. "I'll get rested up," he promises. He reaches for Grandma's coffee mug, and I notice a Post-it note stuck to the table beside it. It springs up off the wood like a cartoon in 3-D. I recognize Grandma's handwriting on it, two words scrawled. I crane my neck to read it—

"Tretch, run and grab those casserole dishes now, please."

I look up. Mom's eyebrows arch. *"Okay,"* I say. I turn to leave, not able to shake the feeling that something's a little off. Why is Dad hugging Grandma like that? Why is Granddad hiding out back? Why do I feel like they're all keeping something from me?

Outside, the remaining two dishes are stacked on top of the Accord. I pull them down, balance them, and carry them back into the kitchen. Everyone has disappeared. Grandma's coffee cup is still there, steam rising; her cards are there, haphazardly stacked; and the Post-it note—it's there, too. I pick it up this time and read.

Multiple myeloma.

"Now what on earth"—I look around, making sure I'm still alone—"is this?" I stick the Post-it back against the tabletop and go to the kitchen window. Outside, Grandma, Mom, and Dad all stand on one side of the fire pit Granddad built. Granddad's standing on the other side. In the middle of them all burns a dull flame, trembling scraps of newspaper and colorful coupon pages beneath it.

Mom sometimes says Granddad has an "artistic temperament," but I'm not sure what that means. To me, right now, he just looks angry—or maybe not *angry*, but definitely annoyed.

He swipes his hand in front of him as if to say *Enough with all this* and turns his back on everyone. Then, hands in his pockets, face pointed at the ground, he ambles off toward his shop in the back corner of the yard.

Mom holds on to Grandma's elbow and Dad shakes his head. *What's wrong?* I wonder. I see Dad's shoulders rise and fall, like he's breathing heavy. He turns away from my mom and Grandma and looks out toward the woods.

I don't know what to think —except that all of this behavior has to have something to do with what was written on that Post-it. *Multiple* whatever. I'll have to get Joe to look it up on his iPhone when he wakes up.

I step away from the window and sit down at the table, memorizing the words on the Post-it. *Multiple myeloma, multiple myeloma, multiple myeloma.* I repeat them over and over, until I know I won't forget. Then I take off through the back door, out across the back porch, past Mom and Dad and Grandma.

"Where you going, Tretch?" Mom asks.

I start jogging. "*Oh*, just to say hey to Granddad!" I call over my shoulder.

The dry grass crunches beneath my feet. There's a light on inside the shop. I can see it through the window, making a shadow of the old tractor parked inside. Granddad has finally retired it, after summer after summer spent making repairs.

I walk through the door of the shop. Granddad is crouched over his workbench in his blue coveralls. He's wiping the surface with a greasy handkerchief.

"Hey, Granddad!" I say.

He jumps, his shoulders and neck snapping back. He turns around. "Well, *heeey*, Junior Junior," he says.

"Sorry to scare you, Granddad."

"It's all right." He nods. "What you doin'?"

"Oh, nothing, Granddad. Just thought I'd run out here and see you."

"Grandma tell you the news?"

I gulp. Here it comes.

"N-n-no," I stutter. *M-m-multiple—*

"Mary's gonna have a baby."

I feel like a balloon has come untied inside me and is slowly letting out air. "*Ooohhh*," I say. Mary the cow is the sweetest, gentlest member of the Farm Farm herd, and her having a calf is news, even if it's not *the* news.

"Should be any day now." Granddad grunts. "You should go have a look at her. Take the truck and go see her if you want—" He turns and gives the workbench another wipe-down.

I clear my throat. "You ready for Christmas, Granddad?"

"Sure am," he answers without turning around. "What about you?"

"Yeah. I think we're about to have the Spaghetti Casserole Feast."

"Mm, that's good." He reaches under the bench and pulls out a large sheet of metal. Then he sets it atop the flat surface of the workbench. The metal plays with the dimness in the shop and casts a tiny burst of light. It reflects off Granddad's chin, his shoulders.

"What you working on, Granddad?" I ask.

" 'Bout to do some metal work, Junior," he says, reaching for his welder's mask. "Gon' get loud. How 'bout you go check on Mary for me? Grab Joe and both of you"—he slides the mask down over his face—"go. Go see 'er."

"Okay, Granddad," I say. "Sounds good."

Mary stands chewing her cud. She chews in rhythm, like she's keeping time, pacing herself like an Olympic cud-chewer. Her belly doesn't look noticeably bigger to me—being a cow, she's already pretty naturally round. But her udders are obviously full, and that's a definite sign of pregnancy.

She burps, throwing off her perfect chewing rhythm.

"Well, Tretch, I sure am glad you woke me up for this," Joe sasses. I know he's mostly kidding, but I can tell he's still exhausted. He even nodded off a couple times on the ride through the woods to the pasture. I sit on the driver's side with the door open and my foot hanging out. Joe's door is open, too. The truck reminds us with a constant dinging.

Ding.

Multiple—

Ding. Ding.

Multiple doors on vehicle—

Ding.

Multiple doors on vehicle open.

Ding.

Multiple—

I shut my door and pull the jacket tight around me. Then I press the brake and turn the key. The truck chokes a little (normal) before it finally revs. I ease it out of park and tap the gas ever so slightly.

"Well, Mary looks fine to me," I say. Joe shuts his door and tips his head against the seat rest, his eyelids fluttering closed. I clear my throat. "Uh, you got your phone on you, Joe?"

"Why?"

"Because I need you to look something up."

"What?" He opens one eye.

"I need you to search 'multiple myeloma' and tell me what it is."

"Mm." He fishes the iPhone in its blue case out of his pocket. "What do you need to know that for?" He presses the screen a couple times.

"I saw it written on that Post-it note in Grandma's kitchen."

Joe presses the screen a few more times. "Uh," he says. "Tretch . . ." Then he looks up, and I know, and I realize that

I *have* known. *You're not stupid*, I remind myself. *Hoping against your better instincts isn't stupid.*

A pulse in my head keeps time on its own.

Joe reads aloud what's popped up on his screen.

But the only word I really hear is *cancer*.

thirteen

All through the Spaghetti Casserole Feast that afternoon, I feel queasy. Apparently, I also don't say much, because Mom keeps asking, "Tretch, everything okay?" I nod and wonder why she's asking me specifically. It's not like I'm the only quiet one at the table. For the most part, nobody's speaking. Everyone just kind of eats, and that is that.

I start looking at my spaghetti really hard and think about *Where the Red Fern Grows*. I read it years ago, but there's that scene when the boy falls on the ax and the kid sees it, and then he has to go home, where his mom is cooking up spaghetti. He takes one look at the slimy red noodles and starts thinking about all the blood and stuff—

This is when I know I'm going to hurl.

Mom and Grandma are clearing the table, Dad is helping Granddad out of his chair by holding on to the crook of his arm, and Joe is doing all he can to avoid falling asleep into the mush on his plate. I push back my chair and walk as smoothly as I can into the guest restroom down the hall. I run water into the sink. My face in the mirror is red along the forehead, little spots of sweat, bloodshot eyes. It's happening.

I kneel to the floor in front of the toilet and retch. Then I see what it looks like inside the toilet bowl and throw up again.

After my two throw-ups, I wipe tears from my eyes and stand slowly. I throw cold water on my face and search in the cabinet for a toothbrush and toothpaste.

There's no toothpaste, but there is baking soda; and the only toothbrush I can find looks to be about forty years old, but I use it anyway, along with the baking soda.

When I step out of the bathroom, my teeth feel like they're coated with wax. I make my way back down the hallway, where Grandma stands washing dishes. I'm not sure where Mom is. Normally she keeps Grandma company. Joe is missing, too, probably gone back to sleep.

"Hey, Grandma," I say. I step up next to her for a moment, but the sight of the spaghetti casserole pan in the sink—gooey cakes of noodle and red hunks of sauce now doused with soapy sink water—makes me feel sick again.

"How's it going, Junior Junior?" Grandma asks.

I take a seat at the table. "Good," I answer. And then, from out of nowhere, I start crying.

I cry too much, I know. But sometimes it feels nice, even if I don't quite understand what it's all about or why I'm doing it. Sometimes it just feels like the only thing to do. And I've never been good at putting it off. I'm trying to keep quiet about it now, but after just one snort, Grandma turns around.

Panic floods her electric-green eyes. "Oh, *Tretch*, oh, baby." The plate she's washing slides from her hands and splashes into the soapy sink bath. She takes the seat next to me and grabs hold of my hand. "What is it, Tretch, dear? What's the matter?"

"Grandma." I'm sobbing now. "Is it back?"

"Is what back?"

"Your c—" I nearly choke on the word. "C-c-cancer."

"Oh, heavens, Tretch." She grabs me by the shoulders and pulls me toward her. I feel a little stubble from her chin along the back of my neck.

It's been almost two years since the doctors said she was clear.

"No, Tretch," she whispers beside my ear. "It's not back. It isn't back."

What? I lift my head and look her in the eyes, everything blurry through my tears. I smile. "Well, good," I say. Some snot catches at the back of my throat as I try to laugh. *But then what's wrong? What does multiple—?*

There are footsteps on the tile behind me, and I turn. Mom stands with hands on her hips. "Tretch," she says. The expression on her face is soft but serious. "Tretch, why don't you walk with me to the Christmas-tree room? I haven't even had a chance to play with the train."

I look back at Grandma, my eyes drying up so that I can see the wetness in hers. "Yes, how 'bout you go play with the train, Tretch?" She pats my back, and I stand. I feel like I'm about six years old.

"I'll be back to help with dishes," I tell her. Grandma smiles. Then I turn and walk alongside Mom down the hallway. She doesn't speak until we're at the door of the Christmas-tree room.

"If anyone ever asks me how much your grandparents love Christmas, I always say, 'Well, they've got a room in the house dedicated to it that stays that way the whole year round, if that means anything.'"

The room is dark at the moment, except for the Christmas-tree lights. But when Mom flips the switch, the whole room bursts into colorful life. The train set roars, encircling the tree and the presents underneath.

Everything is bright. Everything is festive.

Three plastic Santa Clauses line the far side of the room. They're each about four feet tall and wear different suits with individual color schemes: one with a red-and-white suit (Classic Santa), one with a white suit with gold trim (Angel Santa), and one with a long green cape and a crown of holly leaves on his head (Recycling/Composting Santa). Grandma bought them as a set. On a desktop there's a collection of snow globes Grandma and Granddad have gathered over the years—most of them souvenirs from country music festivals—and on the wall hangs a gigantic drawing Granddad did of Santa going surfing. He has fluffy trim around his swim trunks. It used to be my favorite as a kid. I stare at it now. Santa with a slight sunburn on his cheeks. Or maybe that's just how Santa's cheeks are—all rosy and whatnot.

Remember how tan Grandma got with the chemo?

A big shelf in the corner of the room opposite the Santa picture holds old photos from earlier Farm Farm Christmases. There's even one of my dad, nine years old I think, holding up a bright red sweater. He doesn't look super excited about it, and that always makes me laugh. What would Dad have wanted for Christmas when he was nine? I can't even imagine, but surely not a bright red sweater. In that same picture, a man sits off in the corner holding a present of his own. He hasn't opened it yet. And he isn't smiling or looking at the camera. That man is my great-uncle. Uncle Dennis. It's the only picture I've ever seen of him.

Other pictures are of all of us: Grandma, Granddad, Dad, Mom, Joe, and me. There's one of Mom and Dad holding up an ornament with the words OUR FIRST CHRISTMAS on it. There's even one of the two of them in college, visiting Farm Farm for the holidays.

The more I think about it, the more I realize just how much Farm Farm is a part of everything about me. Everything that made me.

I step over the train tracks and jiggle a tiny bell-shaped tree ornament.

"Tretch, what's upsetting you?" Mom asks.

I don't turn around. I just keep messing with the ornament. "Something is happening, and no one will tell me what," I say.

"What do you mean, babe?" She doesn't sound annoyed exactly.

"Everyone seems ... I don't know ... worried or something."

"Are you worried, Tretch?"

"Yes."

"What are you worried about?"

"What I saw on that Post-it note on the kitchen table." I stop jiggling the ornament and turn to face Mom now.

Multiple—

She gives a long sigh. "Tretch—"

"But Grandma said—"

Mom clears her throat. I notice how perfectly still she stands, with her hands in her pockets. "Grandma's fine," she says. For a moment she glances up. I think she might be looking at the angel on top of the Christmas tree. "It's, uh—"

She looks down again. Not at me. Just down.

"It's Granddad this time, Tretch."

I shake my head.

No, I think. *What about everything?* What about how happy we were when Grandma got cleared? What about how two Christmases ago was the best Christmas of them all because we knew we'd be able to have more of them? *Many* more of them. *Many* more Farm Farm Christmas Feasts, *many* more gingerbread-house-building contests, *many* more viewings of *It's a Wonderful Life* and hearing the story of how Grandma once met Jimmy Stewart on a steamboat.

Many more nights sleeping on the floor of Dad's old room.

Many more card games and cups of coffee.

Many more trips out to Granddad's shop to see him.

My throat has a cottony feeling. Like I've swallowed socks. Like I'm about to choke. I am about to choke. *I am choking,* I think, and Mom just stands there watching.

"Now, Tretch," she says, soothing. "It won't be—"

"Is he?" I don't know how to ask. My voice rattles. "How *long*?"

Mom brings a hand to her face. She pulls at the corner of her eye. "There's no way to know for sure, baby," she tells me.

With the words come tears. "But he's got time." She reaches into her pocket and pulls out a tissue. "They said it could even be a few years."

I think the tissue is for her, but Mom steps over the train tracks and brings it up to my nose. She smiles as a couple tears slide down her cheeks. She starts to say "Blow" but instead all she manages is a quiet giggle. It takes me by surprise.

And I start giggling a little, too.

Because we both know I'm too old for her to be doing this for me. Holding a tissue up for me to blow my nose.

Well, she is my mom, after all, I think. *And we are sad. And who really cares, anyway?*

She pulls me close to her and holds me until our shoulders stop shaking, until we are breathing normally again, until our eyes have finally dried.

fourteen

Granddad is out in the shop again.

I hear the sound of welding as I cross the yard, the winter grass crunching under my feet and the white sky above me. All the trees look dead without their leaves, and there's no sound of birds or the traffic rolling by on the highway in the distance. All of it's absorbed by the scratchy echo of the welding, which bounces around on the inside of the shop's tin walls and swallows me. I have to cover my ears and avoid looking too long at the gold spray of sparks trailing from the welder. "What you working on, Granddad?" I call. He doesn't hear.

"Granddad!" I yell. "Hey!"

He keeps welding.

"Granddad!"

The spray of burning metal.

"HEEEY!"

Granddad turns around and faces me with the mask again. He slides it to the top of his head. "Heeey, Junior Junior."

"Whatcha working on?"

He sets the torch down on his carpenter's table. "Aww, just something for the yard."

"Cool," I say. "That's cool, Granddad."

"You 'member Mr. Spenks?"

"Yeah! I remember him." Mr. Spenks is one of Granddad's pals. He and his sons run an auto repair shop not too far from Farm Farm.

"He's been getting me into this sculpture business. Got a whole family of homemade welded reindeer in his yard this Christmas."

"You making a reindeer?"

"Nope. Pair of wings."

I check them out and am surprised to find wings where I hadn't seen wings before. "What for?"

"Thought I'd stick them over on a branch on that big oak out there. They're angel wings, supposed to be. For Dennis."

Uncle Dennis? "Oh," I say. "Well, cool, Granddad." I decide to file that away for a while, to think about it later.

"Oh! Granddad, I meant to tell you! I ran into Mr. Thumb, the man from the 501 Grocery, the other day!"

"Aw yeah? What's he been up to?"

"Well, he said his wife died."

Granddad slumps his head, looking at the wing sort of cockeyed. "I'd heard that," he says.

"But before she did, she made Grandma a scarf. I was supposed to give it to her but I left it at home. It's a nice one, though!"

"Well, that was very thoughtful," Granddad says. "Ye-ea-ah."

I unfold a rusty metal chair and sit down. Granddad eyes the wings. He looks bothered, his eyes all scrunched up and his mouth a straight line. Granddad has really big ears, something I inherited from him. I see some white hairs coming out of one of them and a red line where the strap from the welding mask has rubbed.

Now I have to ask.

"So, Granddad," I say. "You been feeling all right lately?"

"Hm?" He looks at me. "Yeah, I'm feelin' good." He says it like it's an "of course" kind of thing. "Want to see what I made your grandma for Christmas?" He reaches for an old canvas bag sitting below the carpenter's table.

"Absolutely," I tell him. I stand and the rusty chair screeches against the floor. "What is it? You make something?"

"Ye-ea-ah." Granddad reaches into the bag, and a grin forms on his face. He pulls out a book with a leather binding, a *big* square binding, but the book itself is thin. It looks like a scrapbook somebody started, then abandoned a few pages in.

He hands it to me, and I turn it in my hands. There are a bunch of swirly designs on the cover that I love. They're carved into the leather.

I wish I had a phone and could snap a picture and send it to Matt. He would think this was just the coolest.

"Granddad, how'd you do this?" I ask.

"This old thing," he says. He holds up a tool that looks kind of like the tooth-scraper from the dentist—except it has a cord and a plug on the end of it. "The tip of this heats up and lets me carve into the leather. See, it melts it just enough for me to draw lines."

"Oh, wow," I say.

"Smells awful bad while I'm doin' it, though." Granddad chuckles.

I flip the book over so that I can see its cover. On the top, Granddad has drawn in cursive, *Proverbs 30:18–19.* A Bible verse? I think that's kind of unusual, seeing as Grandma and Granddad never go to church. I never even hear them talk about God. There's a Bible sitting on the kitchen bookshelf, though, right next to all Grandma's cookbooks.

"That's your grandma's favorite proverb," Granddad tells me, smiling.

I open up the book. There are only a few pages. The first shows an eagle in the sky, drawn in black ink, with Granddad's signature at the bottom. I recognize it because I know his drawing style so well. (A picture he drew of a sad-looking clown is up on the wall in my bedroom.) I turn the page, and on the back is a Polaroid, glued on. It's the same picture, only in photograph form.

"Your grandma took that picture when we was at Yellowstone."

"Wow," I say. The next page is another drawing, in black ink. It's a weird one, I think. A snake on a rock. There's a Polaroid on the back of it, too. "She take this one?" I ask.

"Nope. That one was me. Took that when I was stationed in Spanish Morocco."

"While you were in the air force?"

"Yep. Snapped it while I was taking a hike with a buddy of mine."

"Oh, wow," I say. I can't say anything else. The next page is another ink drawing of a ship, a big steamer, with ripples around the bottom to show it's on water. It's my favorite one so far. It's the most detailed. And just like the first two, there's a matching photograph on the back, this one too old to be a Polaroid.

"That's the *Compton*. The steamer your great-granddad captained when we lived in Mississippi. Where I met your grandma."

"On a boat?"

"Yep. She was a tour guide. I was takin' a tour."

"Granddad, this is—" I'm going to say *awesome*, but I turn the page, and the next picture stops me.

It's a drawing of my grandma and granddad on their wedding day. I've never seen a picture of them so young. They're holding hands. Granddad looks like Joe in a nice old suit. Grandma has a ribbon in her hair. She's holding flowers.

I turn the page, but there's no picture on the back, not for this one. I don't know what to say. I just have a feeling in my stomach, almost like a sickness, except that I'm not upset. I just think it is beautiful. I think it is the most beautiful thing I have ever seen.

I look back up at my granddad.

"This one I had to do from memory," he says, pointing. There's water in his eyes, but technically he isn't crying, because the tears aren't coming out. Then he blinks a few times and they vanish.

He clears his throat. "So you like it?" He chuckles a little bit more and takes the book from me, closing it and sliding it back into the canvas bag. "I have to keep it out here because, damn, she looks everywhere else!"

"What did it mean, Granddad?" I ask.

"Huh?" He holds the bundle of tarp in his hands.

"The proverb. How did it go with the stuff on the inside?"

"Oh." Granddad sets the tarp down. "Good question." He grabs a scrap of paper sitting on his carpenter's table.

PROVERBS 30:18–19 THERE ARE THREE
THINGS THAT AMAZE ME—NO, FOUR THINGS
THAT I DON'T UNDERSTAND: HOW AN EAGLE
GLIDES THROUGH THE SKY, HOW A SNAKE
SLITHERS ON A ROCK, HOW A SHIP NAVIGATES
THE OCEAN, HOW A MAN LOVES A WOMAN.

It makes sense to me. It's definitely what Granddad has drawn on the pages of the scrapbook.

"Her favorite verse," Granddad says again. "I fudged a little on the 'ship' bit. You see, it's actually a steam*boat*." But it doesn't matter. I look up into his face, red with either cold or embarrassment, and realize he's just taught me what I figure to be the greatest lesson in love. I step forward and hug him tight around the waist. He pats my shoulder.

"Can I keep this?" I ask, holding up the scrap with the verse on it.

"Sure thing, Junior," he says, and I stick it in my pocket.

Granddad spends a minute tidying up his workbench before we make our way across the frosty lawn to the house. He washes his hands with some special soap called Gojo— Grandma calls it "Mojo"—which squirts out in chunky white globs, like cottage cheese, and feels kind of scratchy when you scrub.

When we enter the kitchen, the smell gives me my first notice of the upcoming feast. I know how to identify everything by its smell. Squash casserole (good for summer squash that's been jarred), a honey-basted ham, a turkey, my grandma's dressing, peas, and mashed potatoes. There's even jalapeño cornbread, which Grandma made for the first time at Thanksgiving and liked so much she made it again.

"Spic*aay*," Joe says, tasting it after we're all seated. He chases it with his glass of iced tea, then looks down into his lap. I know he's checking his phone. Every now and then I see his hand drift down to text Melissa, which gets me thinking about Matt and about how Joe once explained love to me. "Like sparks," he'd said.

Sparks. In my head, I see Granddad's welding project, the metallic wings spewing their confetti of flames. I wonder why he wants to hang wings for Uncle Dennis on an oak tree. Then I think, *Could that be the tree Uncle Dennis hanged himself from?* But why would Granddad want to hang the wings from *that*? Why would he want to remind himself?

But he's probably reminded of it already—every time he sees that old tree. Maybe seeing the wings there, attached to it, will give him a better feeling.

"We watching *It's a Wonderful Life* later?" I ask. There isn't much talking going on around the table, with everyone stuffing their mouths with food and lost in thought like I am.

"Oh, *of course*," Grandma says. She reaches over and holds Granddad's hand for a moment, the one that isn't shoveling food with a fork. Granddad's a pretty messy eater. He has some potatoes on his upper lip. Sometimes stuff like that kind of grosses me out, but right now it just makes me smile. And it's good to smile, considering all the things that aren't being said.

There's sickness, and there's sadness.

But the thing is, there's love, too. I try never to forget that.

I'm thinking to myself, *This is the greatest*, because of everything I'm noticing: Dad complimenting Mom's squash casserole, her smiling at him, Joe smiling at the phone in his lap, Grandma wiping Granddad's face. It's a feast of love, a feast of sparks.

My mind can't help but return to Matt.

fifteen

I sit later in my dad's old room holding Joe's iPhone while he takes a shower. I backspace in the search bar where he typed *multiple myeloma* earlier and now type in, *what happens when you fall in love?*

I select the first search result on the screen. It links me to an article. I read my answer in a whisper. "'A mild form of obsession.'"

I tap back into the search bar. "Okay," I say. "One more try." There's no real short way to ask the question, and it takes a couple tries before I finally come up with: *i'm gay. how do i fall out of love with my straight best friend?*

"Whatcha doin, Tretch?"

I jump, dropping Joe's phone onto the bed. I didn't hear the shower turn off.

"Ohh, just searching something." I pick up the phone again and quickly click out of the search. "Nothing important, though."

"Did I get any texts from Melissa?"

"I don't think so. Nothing popped up." I toss the phone to him. He holds it in his palm and stares. He blinks a couple times, then asks, "You ready to go watch *It's a Wonderful Life*?"

"Yes," I say. "Yes, yes, yes."

Every year, on Christmas Eve, we watch *It's a Wonderful Life* as a family—Mom, Dad, Joe, Grandma, Granddad, and me— and every year, when it's over, Grandma winds up telling the story about how she met Jimmy Stewart once, while she was a tour guide on the *Compton*.

This year is no different.

"It was the funniest thing," Grandma says. "I kept saying, 'Daddy, I think that's Jimmy Stewart, the man from *It's a Wonderful Life* and *Mr. Smith Goes to Washington*,' and he just looked at me and shook his head—'Naaah, couldn't be'— but it sure was! And I got the signature to prove it."

"Where is the signature, Grandma?" Joe asks. "I'd like to look at it."

It's funny. Now that Joe mentions it, I realize, as much as we've heard about it, neither of us has ever actually *seen* the Jimmy Stewart autograph.

Granddad starts cackling, and Grandma shoots him a look through squinty eyes.

"What?" I ask. "Why are you laughing, Granddad?"

Granddad shakes his head. "She lost it," he says. "She cain't find it nowhere."

Grandma slaps him on the arm. "Now, wait a second. Just because I haven't seen it in a while doesn't mean it's lost," she says. "Probably just somewhere in that cedar chest with all the rest of that old stuff."

"Oh, boy," Dad says. "That thing would take *years* to riffle through."

"Oh, phooey." Grandma waves her hand. "I bet I could find it *tonight* if I wanted to."

"I'll help you look, Grandma," I volunteer.

"Let's do it, Junior Junior." The couch sighs as Grandma stands. I follow her down the hall, a few steps past the dark kitchen, into the bedroom.

In all these years, I've never seen the inside of the old cedar chest. It sits at the foot of Grandma and Granddad's bed and, as far back as I can remember, has always been locked.

When I was a kid, I used to climb on top of it and get in trouble. You weren't supposed to climb on top of the cedar chest because some of the wood was chipped, and every scuff from my little-kid shoes only chipped away at it more. Now it's missing some pretty clean strips, the gold-brown cedar sheen scratched off to reveal its inner bark. I give it a soft rub with my forefinger, risking splinters.

Grandma rummages in the drawer of her nightstand and pulls out the key. She sticks it in the tiny silver lock and turns. I imagine the sensation of gold light rising from some kind of locked-away treasure. But it's all imagination. All I can really see when Grandma lifts up the hood is paper. Notebook-paper scraps, newspaper pieces, some clippings with pictures, envelopes with stamps in the corners. Chaos. Grandma plunges her hands into it, scooping through, then looks up.

"Tretch, will you get the light?" she asks.

"Sure thing." I go to the wall and flip the light switch. The room brightens, and the walls turn a soft peach color. The heaps of paper inside the chest reflect a kind of glow, and I'm less scared to dip my hands in. I kneel down by Grandma's side then, and together we drag our hands through the dry muck. I can't help but picture dumping a pitcher full of wet glue into the mix and making a gigantic vat of papier-mâché.

I look at the scrap I'm holding in my hand. It's a newspaper article: *The King Dies*, it reads. Underneath the headline, Elvis stands with legs splayed and hip cocked, holding a microphone, his mouth stretched wide. "Whoa," I remark. Grandma nods.

"Not a day goes by," she says, "when I don't think about him."

I find several articles on the integration of schools, and one article on another death. The death of another King, actually. He looks somber in his picture. The headline reads *A Nation in Tears*. I hold it out to her. Again, she nods.

"You know, my daddy couldn't stand Martin Luther King. Hated what he stood for. Of course, Daddy was a racist most of his life." She pauses. "Dr. King died a week before he him self passed." Grandma pushes past a jumble of opened letters and torn envelopes. My own hands have reached something hard below a thick stack of metal-ringed notebooks. I knock my knuckles against it. Grandma sighs. "But, you know, I was sitting with him while he died—Daddy, that is, not Dr. King—and somehow he got to talking about it all. About how unfortunate it was that he had died. I said, 'Daddy, what made you change your mind so sudden?' and he smiled. He said, 'I guess I've been realizing we're all just people, Teeney. We all gotta raise our kids, watch our loved ones get old and go. We all been made by the same God, ain't we?'"

I look over at Grandma as she remembers everything. I know her father died of a stroke. He'd had several of them, one after the other, really quickly, and he died in the hospital. I search for some tears in her eyes, but I don't even see one tiny speck.

"And I told him I agreed." She slides the fragile newspaper

from my hand. "Between you and me, I think Daddy might have had a talk with God sitting there in the hospital." A smile spreads across Grandma's face. She places the article back in the chest, and I watch her stir it into the mix. It becomes just another sheet of paper, floating around in there with Elvis, clippings of my dad, photos of me and Joe, marriage announcements, restaurant menus, everything of some kind of value to Grandma. And somewhere in there, maybe, is a signed piece of paper from Jimmy Stewart.

"Do you remember what he signed it on, Grandma?" I ask. She laughs. "Hell if I know, JJ."

After a little while, Grandma is ready to give up. I'm still searching beneath the stacks of spiral-bound notebooks. They're now forming a big pile at my side.

"What are all these?" I flip one open and stare at a scrawl in blue pen that covers an entire lined page. The handwriting is small but neat.

"Oh," Grandma says. She picks one up. "These belonged to your great-uncle. Journals he kept. It was something the doctor asked him to do." She weighs it in her hand, and for a second acts as though she might flip open the cover. "Your granddad read them all, after Dennis passed away. I don't know why. At the end of the day, it just tortured him. In a way, I guess, it was like keeping him around, like we might be able to ask him why he did what he did, you know? Why he chose to end it."

She places the notebook back on top of the stack.

"I don't think he ever got any answers, though." Grandma braces herself against the corner of the chest and stands slowly. "Better put those back at the bottom where you found 'em, JJ. Your granddad told me to never throw them away, but if it had been up to me, I would've." She straightens her back.

"Can I look through the chest some more?" I ask. I'm not sure if she'll mind or not.

"Well sure, sweetheart," she says. "But don't be too long. We still got gingerbread houses to make."

I slide the topmost notebook off the stack and stick it under my shirt.

"Oh, I won't be long," I say.

Joe and I win the gingerbread-house-building contest as always.

We're awarded two homemade candy canes, about which Grandma whoops, "Now *those* were an adventure to make!" Granddad slaps his forehead. "I just hope they taste all right," he admits.

Joe and I take one lick of our candy canes each when we get upstairs and fly straight to the bathroom.

"*Blech!*" I spit. "Sour!" We toss them into the wastebasket.

Joe gargles with some water from the sink. "I guess it's the thought that counts," he says, water still pooled at the back of his throat.

I make sure the candy canes head to the bottom of the wastebasket while Joe spits. When I stand up, he's leaning against the sink, texting.

"I think I'm gonna take my shower now," I say.

"All riiight," Joe replies. His head is somewhere else. He slides outside the door, his thumbs still moving along the iPhone's tiny keypad.

I shut the door and reach into my overnight bag, where I've stowed Uncle Dennis's journal for the time being. Then I pull open the shower curtain and turn on the water. I can't take too long, I know, but I've bought myself some time.

The journal sits flat in my hands. I don't know whether to start from the beginning or to select a page at random. Its bright red cover gleams from the overhead lighting. I'm paranoid about getting it wet.

I open the journal to the first page. The entry is dated *August 12, 1976.*

> *Well, home from the doctor. He didn't help*
> *much, like I expected, but that's okay . . .*

This feels wrong. It feels wrong to be reading this.

> *He did say something that kind of made me*
> *think. About living and being alive. He said,*

*"You know, Mr. Farm . . ." and I told him
he could just call me Dennis. "You know,
Dennis," he said. "You don't have to feel
guilty for being alive through all this. Some
people feel guilty for surviving. Some people
actually feel so guilty about surviving that,
ultimately, they make sure they don't." I
thought he was going to start talking to me
about suicide, but he didn't. Instead he said,
"They force themselves to go through life like
zombies. They never let themselves feel again.
They don't accept love or kindness. Nothing
except anger and fear. Is that how you want to
go through life, Dennis?" I answered like I knew
he wanted me to, said, "No, Doctor." Then he
nodded and said, "Well, then, you have to
forgive yourself." I said, "Forgive myself for
what?" And he said, "Surviving." That's when
the time ran out and I had to leave . . .*

I thumb a couple pages over, skimming them as I go. Most
of the entries look like reports from Uncle Dennis's psychia-
trist visits. A couple times he mentions medicines they're giving
him. In one passage, a word catches my eye, an unusual word.

Bear.

So I told Doc about a good memory I have
of Bear.

I back up and read the whole page.

I mentioned Bear to the doctor today for the
first time. He said he'd heard mention of him
from Richard. Apparently Richard said
something to him about me losing a friend in
battle and how that was part of the reason I'm
having some trouble. I didn't talk about Bear's
death, though. I won't write about it, either.
Doc says don't rush thinking about those kind
of things. All that, all the grief and everything,
just takes time to process. It'll happen on its
own, he says. So I told Doc about a good
memory I have of Bear. The time he and I left
camp to go on that hike to the top of Sound
Mountain and ended up in a little trouble. We
didn't realize how long it would take to get to
the top, and by the time we got back it was
dark and rainy. Sarge was pretty pissed off,
too. "Y'all want to go off and hold hands, do
it a little closer to camp next time," he said.
That embarrassed us both pretty bad. We

didn't go on another adventure for a while,
but that had been a good one. My best
memory from that hike is when Bear's boot
slid off a rock he was propped on and got
stuck in some deep mud. The mud was so
deep. It nearly swallowed him up to his calf.
When he finally pulled it out it made a sound
like a suction cup, and we both laughed. Bear
was mad because he said he was probably
going to chafe on the way back.

I flip a couple pages over. There's a good bit on this Bear
guy, though Uncle Dennis never brought up anything specific
about his friend's death—other than to point out again that
Bear was dead and that he was sad because of it.

Today Doc said to me, "Dennis, Bear died,
and there's nothing you can do about it
now, and there was nothing you could do about
it then." I said, "I know, I'm not stupid, Doc,"
and he said, "But that doesn't mean you won't
see him ever again." I said I hoped he was
right, but that I wasn't gonna rely on it.

In a couple entries, he leaves out any mention of Bear.

Tonight, I am supposed to write about
something I would love to do that I've never
done. Doc's orders.

I've been thinking about how, since it's
cold now and the pond is iced over, I'd like to
go down through the woods on a clear night,
sit on top of that ice and look up at the stars.
I think about how perfect that would be.
That would make everything feel okay, I
think. Even if it was just right in that second,
everything would feel all right. Maybe some
night I'll do it if I get the chance.

It's a weird entry.

But, in a way, they're all weird entries.

This one just seems especially weird because Uncle Dennis sounds happy. Every time I've heard about him, the little bit Dad shared, or even the very little bit Grandma shared (Granddad never talks about him), it was enough to make me think he couldn't even imagine happiness. He was that far gone. But here he is, imagining it. Here, it looks like there's some hope.

But Uncle Dennis is already dead, just like that kid from Samsanuk is already dead. Even if there was hope at one point, it's all gone now.

I close the notebook and hop in the shower, thinking maybe I've done a bad thing.

· ·

That night, we all go to bed happy. Just like every Christmas Eve night I can remember. Dad calls up the stairs to me and Joe and says, "G'night, guys!" Mom says, "Night, boys. I love y'all!"

"*Night!*"

"*Night!*"

Grandma and Granddad have long gone to bed. Last, I say good night to Joe. I'm lying on the pullout mattress that sits below my dad's old bed. Joe and I used to wrestle over who got the bed. But Joe always won, so now I guess it's just tradition that I get the pullout and he gets the bed. I like the pullout, anyway.

"Mer-ry Christmas, Mr. Potter!" Joe calls down to me.

"Ha," I laugh. "Merry Christmas, Joe."

sixteen

The next day, we all sit inside the Christmas-tree room and open presents. I get some jeans and a new polo shirt from Grandma, which is the exact same thing Joe gets except that Joe's is a deep green and mine is a bright pink with some white lines on it.

"*Ooh*, Grandma!" I say. "I love it!"

I also get a new drawing from Granddad. This one is of a woman·in a frilly short skirt with a big feather hat, walking a tightrope. She is holding an umbrella high over her head as she sticks out one leg, demonstrating her impeccable balance to the circus-going crowd. Joe gets a drawing, too, of an elephant carrying a woman (the same woman, I think, as the one who's walking the tightrope in my drawing). They're both framed and behind glass where nothing can tarnish them. When I open mine, I hold it tightly to my chest.

From Joe, I get a little leather-bound journal.

"Wow, Joe," I tell him, fanning the blank pages. "Thank you."

Joe shrugs. "You read so much. You should try your hand at writing, Tretch-o."

I know the kind of writing he means isn't the same as the kind of writing Uncle Dennis put in his own blank book. But I can't help but think of our great-uncle, and how he got his journal under such a different circumstance. I'm the lucky one here.

Then comes the big present—from Mom and Dad—an iPod. I slide it out of its case and hold it delicately, scared I might crush it in my excitement. "Oh my gosh," I say. *"Thank you."*

"Merry Christmas, Tretch," Mom says, smiling.

I look at Dad, and he winks.

When it comes time for Grandma to open her present from Granddad, I hold my breath. The scrapbook with its leather binding emerges from beneath newspaper wrapping. I think she might cry out and say, "Oh, Richard!" or something but she doesn't. She's silent. She holds it in her hands for a few seconds and doesn't look up. But when she does look up, her eyes meet with Granddad's, and they swap a smile. It makes me so happy and so sad at the same time, because I want it to always be like this. But it won't be, it can't be, and I know this.

I feel the thought of an end tugging at me, yanking me out of what is now. *Hold fast to that which is good, Tretch. Hold fast to that which is now.*

Right now, Grandma is looking up. "Well, how 'bout that?" she says. "Pretty neat, Rich."

Granddad laughs. "Mhmm." He probably figured she wouldn't show much emotion. That wouldn't be the Grandma thing to do. He probably knew she would take it just like she took every other present she received—with a kind remark and a smile. But he also has to know it means the world to her. He understands it, and she understands it, and they just smile at each other and laugh, and say things like "That's pretty neat" and "Mhmm."

I think that must be what it's like to be in love and to have been in love for a long time.

We eat our Christmas Eve leftovers, marking the end of the Christmas Feast Marathon, and leave the gift wrapping scattered around the Christmas-tree room. We'll clean up later, once the buzz has died, and Grandma will finalize it all by saying, "*Well*, that's that. All the preparation and it's over before you know it."

But for now we're eating and laughing and talking, and nobody watching us could tell Granddad is sick, or that anyone is worried, because right now we aren't feeling anything bad. It's all good, really, just perfectly all good.

Granddad even surprises us by telling a story about Uncle Dennis that makes us all smile. One about how one time when they were kids they went exploring in the woods behind their house. Granddad had taken his BB gun and Uncle Dennis hadn't taken anything. "I thought I might be able to shoot me some squirrel or something," Granddad says to us now. "But Dennis, he had something else in mind. He had been lookin' through one of those View-Master things all morning. Richard, you remember you had one of those?"

"I did." Dad nods. "So did the boys."

"The binocular-looking thing where you click the switch and the pictures change?" Joe asks.

"Yes!" Granddad says. "Dennis had been clicking through it and looking at all those sliding pictures. There was this one that he loved—a picture of a waterfall. And Dennis was just dying to see something like it, something that wasn't a picture, you know? He wanted to see the real thing, a real live waterfall. And normally, you know, he wouldn't have gone out into the woods with me. He hated to see me shoot anything, even if it was just a little squirrel or something. But it had rained the day before, and Dennis thought we might be able to see a real live waterfall if we looked in the right spot. Dennis said, 'I bet the trench is filled up, Rich. If it is, it's gotta flow out to somewhere.'

"So we went looking for the outlet. I saw a few squirrel along the way, but I didn't shoot them since I knew Dennis didn't like to watch that. We walked for a while, following this big long trench all the way across our land. Dennis was right— it had filled up from the rain, and there was water rushing through it. And I hoped so badly we would get to some kind of deposit somewhere so Dennis could see a real waterfall. We walked and walked. We crawled under some barbed wire, realized we weren't even on Daddy's land anymore, and kept walking. Finally, Dennis turned to me and said, 'You hear that, Rich?' I listened, and sure enough, I heard it. Sound of water splashing. Then Dennis took off! The ground started to slope all suddenly, and I reckon Dennis must have tripped. He was running full steam ahead through all kinds of prickly brush, and when I caught up to him, he was cut up on his hands and his face.

"But he had found it. There it was. Right in front of us, a real live waterfall. Not an especially big thing, of course, but it was there. And we stood looking at that thing, feeling water splash up from the bottom of the trench. It couldn't have meant more to two people in the world than it meant to me and Dennis right then, not even two men thirstin' in the desert, I swear."

Granddad folds his hands. Grandma reaches over and curls her own hand around his. I remember Uncle Dennis's journal, still stowed away in my overnight bag upstairs. *I have to return it*, I think.

That night, we wreck the gingerbread houses and munch on them until we can't munch anymore. Joe has some frosting on his top lip, and I don't tell him about it. But I laugh every time I look at him.

He doesn't notice until later, when we're brushing our teeth.

"Tretch, you doofus, why didn't you *tell* me?" He nudges my shoulder with his elbow, squirting Colgate Total Whitening onto his toothbrush.

Then the phone rings.

I look at Joe. "What time is it?"

Joe shrugs. "Maybe ten? I don't know."

"Kind of late," I say. I spit toothpaste into the sink and rinse it from my mouth.

"Tretch!" Mom calls up the stairs. "Phone's for you!"

Joe raises his eyebrows at me. My cheeks burn, and my heart starts to pound. I don't want to, really shouldn't, get my hopes up.

But who else could it be?

I jump down the stairs, looking probably a little too happy.

Mom's at the foot. "It's Matt. He's calling from New York and wants to wish you a merry Christmas." She smiles. "You'll have to talk in the kitchen. I couldn't find the cordless."

My chest tightens, and I wonder if I might just snap from all this excitement and all this trying-to-remain-cool simultaneously.

It's only a friend calling, I remind myself.

He's only a friend.

Doing a thing friends do.

I bound into the kitchen. The phone rests on the floor at the end of its long, curly cord. I pick it up and speak, a little loudly at first.

"Hello?"

"Hey, Tretch!"

The sound of his voice is enough to erase any calm I may have collected. I can't hold back. Everything bursts out of me.

"Matt! What's up? I miss you! Merry Christmas!"

Matt chuckles, and I think I can hear traffic in the background. Big-city traffic. New York traffic.

"Not too much, Tretch. We, uh, just went to look at the tree in Rockefeller Center."

There's a shuffle then, a kind of fuzzy movement sound.

"Matt?" I say. "Can you hear me?"

"I—" he says. And then there's a fade.

"Ugh!" I wrap the phone cord around my fingers. I wait. More shuffles, then finally—

"*Okay!* Can you hear me *now*?"

"Yes!" I shout. "Yes! I can hear you!"

"Okay, good, we're in the cab now."

"Oh, okay, *cool*." *A cab.* "How's the tree? Is it as big as it looks on TV?"

"Oh, Tretch, it's awesome. You would totally flip out over it."

"Seriously?" I realize I'm nodding my head furiously, then stop. But maybe Matt's nodding, too.

"Oh yeah, it's su*perb*!"

"Awesome."

"Yeah."

"Well . . ." I realize the phone cord is cutting off circulation to my fingers. "How's the city life?"

"Uh-mazing."

I look out the kitchen window. All dark and quiet on the Farm Farm front. No traffic. No people. And what life there is moves at the pace of frozen molasses.

"I bet," I say.

"Yeah." Matt gives a quiet laugh. "Funny I still have your grandparents' number from last summer."

That makes me smile. "Yeah, you called just about every night, I think. I'm surprised you don't have it memorized by now."

I'm kidding, and he knows. He laughs for a few seconds, and all the while, my heart is fluttering in my chest. All my breaths come hard. It feels like it's been *so long*, when really it's been less than a week.

Granted, I have filled a healthy portion of that time thinking about him.

And I guess he's been thinking about me, too. Maybe not as much. But at least a little.

"Well, Tretch," he says, "I've got some news."

"Oh yeah?" I say. "What's up?"

"Guess what my Christmas present was!"

"I thought it was tickets to *Hedwig and the Angry Inch*?"

"No, there's more. Much more."

"What, Matt? *What?*"

"We're moving back!"

All of a sudden, my knuckles feel prickly. I look down and notice the cord again, wrapped too tightly. Painfully.

"What?"

"To New York! Dad, Pop, and me! We're moving back!"

"W-wh—?" I can't get it out. I don't know what to say. "Wh-what, Matt? Say it again."

"Oh, sorry, Tretch, am I losing you again? The service is, like, super spotty."

"Yeah, yeah," I say. "Could you just—?"

I know I need to clear my throat, or close my eyes, or *something*. The tears are coming on fast. But what I feel like I need above all else, what I want anyway, is silence.

"Tretch?"

I can't speak yet.

"Tretch?"

I swallow.

"Tretch, did I lose you again?"

No, Matt. I lost you.

I clear my throat. "No, no. That's, uh—that's big news, Matt!" I clear my throat again. "That's exciting, really. That's really . . ." I trail off.

There's only silence on the other end.

"Matt, are you there?"

Silence.

"*Matt?*" It comes up with a choke. *Oh no. Please, no.*

"Tretch?"

"Yeah! Hey!"

"Sorry again for this service."

"No, it's *okay*." I breathe. "It's *okay*, Matt—"

"Oh, gosh. Tretch, I'm losing you again. This is so—"

Again, there's silence.

I stand waiting for him to get through it, though. I stand holding the phone for a long time, long after I start to realize he's hung up. Given up.

"Lost him," I say. "Lost him."

I let the raveled cord loosen. Then I release my hand, all red-knuckled and white-fingered. I try to place the phone back in its cradle, but it doesn't stick and falls off again, hitting me in the shoulder and clanging against the hard kitchen floor.

"Tretch?" Mom calls from the living room. "Everything all right?"

"Everything's all right," I say. "Just gonna hit the sack, I think."

"Okay," she says. "All good on Matt's end?"

"Yeah, he's loving New York," I tell her. "As usual."

That's all I can admit to her, or anyone, right now.

seventeen

It's late in the night. No longer Christmas. Joe's asleep on the bed above me, but I can't sleep. Finally, I realize there's no point in trying.

I need air.

I need space.

I need a place where I can scream or cry without anyone hearing, without anyone asking questions.

I sneak down the stairs, not wanting to wake anyone, and finally I push out the back door. Before I notice much of anything else, I'm traipsing through the woods with my fleece jacket pulled tight around my stomach. The zipper on it is broken, so I hold it closed. The wind scrapes against my face, as I dip under low branches and hop over icy patches along the dirt path, but I don't mind it; it feels like something I deserve. I keep moving, even when my jeans get snagged on some briars. I keep walking until they pull free and I feel the stabs they've left. They don't hurt, though, not that bad.

Everything feels different in the dark.

I can't feel the woods anymore. They're behind me. The night sky is opening up with brilliant stars and a brilliant moon, a few dusty clouds hanging between them. I hug the jacket tighter to me and walk quickly, stretching my legs out, the ground steepening slowly as I go. When at last it flattens out, I look out across the meadow.

Matt, you have to see this.

I can see cows off in the distance, crouched motionlessly in sleep. I can see the barn, half empty of hay by this time of year. Then, as I tip my face forward, following the ground's downward slope, I see what I've come for. It's winking its moonlight reflection at me. I brace against gravity, walking the steep slope that leads me to it. I stand on its frosty bank, looking over the completely iced surface.

Safe, I think. *Surely safe.*

I slide one foot out onto the slick surface. I am scared to leave the bank entirely. What was it Uncle Dennis said again? I try to remember exactly. *Lie down on the ice and look up at the stars.* Something like that. *And then you'll know every-thing will be okay.*

I want to know this.

I want to know this for sure.

I set my butt down on the ice and start to push off with my hands, the ice sticking to my palms so that I have to peel them away.

Should've worn gloves, I think. Then suddenly I feel the first give. The ice shudders beneath me, and slush rises up around my fingers. I feel a shivery wetness on the butt of my jeans. I realize there is nothing I can do.

The ice is giving way.

I budge, just one slight push with my heels back toward the bank. It's enough. The ice beneath me breaks in, tips me for-ward, and I slide feetfirst into the water as if this has all been planned. Dennis's words. Matt's words. My actions. I'm mid-breath when water slams into my face. I swallow a portion, rancid-tasting and freezing in my throat. Deeper than I thought it would be.

There's a pounding in my chest. *That's your heart,* I think, *all broken up but beating anyways. It's trying to save you. Feel it go, Tretch. Feel your heart, working harder than ever.* It is working to save me, and everything else is working to save it. I can feel the blood leaving my hands and feet to rush toward it. All for protection. My body is going numb but I'm thinking,

This is right, this is supposed to happen. Everything is working like it's supposed to. But I'm still underneath. I'm still freezing. And I'm really going to die if I don't push myself up.

I give it a try, but no use. No strength. I'm all heavy.

I gasp and my body fills with more water. I am fighting and I am losing. I look up, and there it is. Heaven lights up in the night sky. But in front of it, like an obstacle I have to face before I get there, is the statue of William Griggers, the Warmouth soldier, the one that usually stands in front of the courthouse. *What's it doing here?* Only—wait a second— that's not what I'm seeing at all. It's the boy from Samsanuk, the one whose name I refused to read in the paper, the one who killed himself because it had all gotten too big for him, too heavy.

Then the Samsanuk kid shape-shifts and becomes a grown man I recognize instantly. With droopy shoulders and a sad smile, scraggly hair growing from his chin, a big nose, dark hair.

Uncle Dennis.

I want to call out to him, *HELP!* But nothing comes.

HELP, PLEASE! I'M DROWNING!

Then the figure shifts again, and there's a splash, and two arms wrap around me. I am pulled up and let out a breath that grates the insides of my throat like I'm spitting up cold rocks. I look up and see heaven as it closes up again. Just the night sky now. Brilliant stars, brilliant moon. Someone holds me. I realized I'm being carried. "Who?" I ask. But the figure won't stop speaking. "Tretch," it's saying, "Tretch, Tretch, Tretch, Tretch . . ."

"Who . . ." I try again.

"Tretch, Tretch, Tretch . . ."

"*Who?*"

"Tretch, Tretch, Tretch . . ."

Dad carries me into the dark house. He sets me down on the bathroom floor, where he helps me out of my wet clothes and wraps me in towels. Once I'm dried off and a little warmer, he turns on the bathwater and makes me get in the tub. His whole body is shaking.

"Are you cold?" I ask.

He looks at me, eyes tired. "No," he says. "Tretch, why did you . . . What were you . . . Were you . . ." He shakes worse suddenly, one big shake rattling up his back and snapping between his shoulders. Even his neck quivers.

"I—" I start. But what can I say? "I'll show you." I know I'll have to tell him about Uncle Dennis's journal, about stealing it and reading it. Once I hop out of the bath, body temperature back to normal, I tiptoe into my room and slide it out from inside my overnight bag. I don't know how I find the exact entry, but I do. I find it instantly. I read it aloud to him.

"Here's what it says, Dad. It says, 'I've been thinking about how, since it's cold now and the pond is iced over, I'd like to go down through the woods on a clear night, sit on top of that ice and look up at the stars. I think about how perfect that would be. That would make everything feel okay, I think. Even if it was just right in that second, everything would feel all right.'"

He's silent for a while, then he reaches for the notebook. I let him have it.

"Son," he says, running his finger down the metal spine, "I think you need to go to bed."

"Dad, I'm fine," I tell him. "I promise."

"I think you need to rest."

Tears well in my eyes. "Dad, I'm *okay*."

"Tretch." He puts his face in his hand. "Please just—" He swallows. "Go get some rest."

I want to go before I see him cry. I am scared to see him cry. He doesn't understand that I really will be okay. Sure, I did something a little crazy, but it was mostly by accident.

"I'm sorry, Dad. It was stupid."

"Tretch."

I am tired of hearing my name.

"Dad, I wasn't trying to—" I don't know how to finish the sentence. *I wasn't trying to kill myself?* But I wasn't. He waves his arm to shush me.

"Go," he says, still looking down. He points toward the stairs.

I look behind me, then back at him. I don't want to leave him sitting there on the bathroom floor wondering, worried more than anything, now, about me. I turn and walk toward the stairs, feeling sore under my arms from where he lifted me. And sick to my stomach from what I'm feeling. Upstairs, I leave the door to Dad's old room open, while I position myself on the pullout mattress in a way that will let me see the bathroom light go out. If it goes out, I will know Dad is going back to bed. If it goes out, I can be put at ease.

But it stays on.

As far as I know, it stays on for the rest of the night.

eighteen

When I get out of bed, after what feels like no sleep at all, I find Dad sitting on the living room couch. He's next to Mom, sipping coffee, and I can tell right away that he hasn't told her.

I have to reckon that sometimes you just let things go.

Dad isn't going to tell Mom, and I'm not going to tell Joe. And what even happened, anyway? If love is a mild form of obsession, and obsession is just some form of crazy, then *yes*, maybe I acted a little crazy. But I never thought, never expected—I explained it to him, didn't I? *I just wanted to feel like it would all be okay.*

But does he understand?

When I enter the room, Dad looks up. Even though he's hiding it from Mom, I can tell he's concerned.

"Morning, Tretch," he says.

"Morning, Dad."

Mom is reading the paper. She flips a page and says good morning to me, too. Everything is normal. For now, everything is okay. Yes, Granddad is sick, Matt is leaving, I almost died, and Dad is probably wondering if I'm suicidal. But Mom is reading the paper, and Joe is still sleeping, and I imagine Grandma is in the kitchen about to pour herself some coffee. In a moment, Granddad comes in from his morning routine to announce that Mary the cow still hasn't had her calf.

"Don't know when she's gonna have that thing," he tells us. "Sure thought it'd be by now—"

I don't want to leave. Because leaving will push my story forward. Leaving will put me one step closer to Matt's last day in Warmouth. Leaving will put one more Farm Farm Christmas behind me. But what can you do to stop it?

Around eleven o'clock, after Joe has woken and we've packed up the car, it's time to say good bye.

"See you on New Year's, my dear," Grandma says, kissing me on the cheek.

"See ya on New Year's, Grandma," I reply. Granddad stands off to the side, smiling. He reaches out his hand for a high five, and when I give it to him, he says, "*There* ya go!"

I slide into the backseat next to Joe. Dad flashes a glance in the rearview. "Tretch, you need your CD player?" he asks. "I stuck it up here in the glove compartment."

"Oh," I say. "No, sir. I'm fine."

"Katy, hand him his CD player."

Mom turns her head. "Tretch, do you want it?"

I shake my head.

Dad won't let it go, though. "Well, of course he wants his music—he's Tretch, isn't he?" He reaches over to the glove compartment and yanks it open.

"Okay, okay," Mom says. She takes out the CD player and hands it to me. "It'll be nice to start using your iPod, won't it, Tretch?"

"It will be," I say.

I slide the headphones over my ears and press the play button, but nothing happens. I try again. "I think the batteries are dead," I say, pulling the headphones off.

We've already started down the driveway. Dad turns his head. "We can stop and get you some on the way home," he says.

I shake my head. "Dad, *no*."

"You sure?" he asks. "It would just be a quick stop." He presses on the brake.

"Dad," I say, looking hard at him. "I am fine. I swear."

"Richard, he's *fine*," Mom says. But Dad's eyes are locked onto mine, searching them.

Really, I mouth.

Dad nods. *Open it*, he mouths back. Then he turns around and lets off the brake. The car rolls into motion. I glance at Joe—his eyes are closed, his forehead resting against the window.

I pop open the CD player.

Inside is a tiny sliver of folded paper. It looks like a fortune from a fortune cookie. I unfold it and find a short note written in blue ink.

> *Tretch, I promise. Everything is going to be*
> *OK. I love you.*
> —Dad

I glance up at the rearview mirror, and sure enough, Dad is looking. I nod. He blinks once and looks away. I close my eyes and tip my head against the headrest. A single tear slides from the corner of my eye and makes its way down my cheek. I think about Grandma and Granddad, probably just now sitting back down at the kitchen table to finish their coffees. I think about Matt and his dad, maybe they're ice skating in Rockefeller Center or something. For a second, I wonder about Nana and Papa, about Christmas in Dallas with my cousins on Mom's side. I think about that stupid *Chitty Chitty Bang Bang* DVD, my new polo, the painting of the tightrope walker, my journal. I'm excited about using my iPod. I wonder if Lana

Kramer ever receives any presents on December twenty-fifth as a kind of consolation, since Hanukkah's already over by then.

I think for a second about Amy Sinks's New Year's dance, how I'm still kind of looking forward to it, even though everything has changed.

It's like the next few days don't really happen. Or they're so empty they don't even count as days. I get through all the post-Christmas routines. I download songs onto my iPod. I play video games with Joe when he's not with his girlfriend. I don't leave the house unless it's with another family member. I don't hear from Matt.

I'm close to convincing myself that the whole thing out on the ice never happened. It feels like some kind of dream, some kind of bad dream, most likely brought on by bad news upon bad news upon bad.

Finally, I can see my parents starting to worry that I'm not leaving the house, so I make my way to Mabel's. I wonder if Amy knows that Matt's leaving, and this seems one way to find out.

She seems happy to see me, and doesn't seem sad at anything, so I'm guessing she doesn't know. I don't say much more than hi to her, then I bury myself in my book.

I lose track of time until Amy reaches over and pours more coffee into my mug. "Wow, I never knew you were such a reader," she says. "Or such a coffee drinker, for that matter."

I'm only on my third cup.

And I'm one page away from finishing *A Separate Peace.*

"Oh, *yeah*," I say. "I drink coffee. And I read. I drink coffee and read." I look up at her. "And that's pretty much it, Amy."

"Well, don't forget dancing," she says, flashing a smile. "I can't wait to see you bust a move at the party tomorrow."

The door to Mabel's chimes open, and Amy saunters over to the counter to grab a menu. The customer is an old man, kind of scraggly looking, with holes in his pants. He wears a beanie hat kind of like Landon's except it looks like it's never been washed. His jacket looks good, though, slick so rain can slide off but thick enough to keep him warm. He reminds me of Mr. Thumb, if a little more sprightly looking. I tug at the scarf around my neck, tucked down the front of my shirt.

The old man stomps over behind Amy as she leads him to the table across from mine. He sits down facing me. *Well, this is awkward*, I think, looking down at my book so fast my neck pops. I hear Amy ask, "Anything to eat, sir?"

"Oh, no thank you, ma'am," the old man says. "Just a coffee will be good."

By the time Amy returns with his mug and the coffee, I've finished. I flip the back cover closed and shut my eyes. *God*, I think.

"A doozy, isn't it?"

I look up.

The old man is staring at me. And it isn't until then that I realize he's the Jim Cho's Santa Claus. He smiles, his cheeks still pink from the cold. His teeth are yellow.

"Oh," I say. "Yeah, I hated it."

"*Really?* Why?"

"Too sad."

The Jim Cho's Santa Claus nods. "I remember it that way."

"You read *A Separate Peace*?" I'm surprised. The Jim Cho's Santa Claus doesn't strike me as the kind of guy who'd be interested in the story of two boys—best friends—who basically ruin each other's lives.

"Years and years ago." Santa stretches his arms. "But I remember pieces. I remember that it was sad."

"It's not like it's a bad book," I say. "It's just . . . hmm . . ." I can't think of a word to describe it.

Santa shakes his head. "You're disgusted by it!"

"Yeah," I say. "Maybe that's it."

"And that's okay!" Santa assures me. "It's good to have strong reactions to things. Especially books." He eyes the second title in my stack. "What you got there?"

"*On the Road.*"

"Aha." He nods, his eyes closing like he's meditating. "Now *that's* a wonderful book."

"Really?"

"Oh yes, one of my favorites." He opens his eyes. "Yes, sir, I did my first cross-country hitchhike after I finished that book. I quit school, told my family I loved them, and stuck out my thumb. Just a couple of weeks later I was staring all bleary-eyed at the Pacific Ocean."

I'm a little stunned. Who would have thought the Jim Cho's Santa Claus was a professional hitchhiker in the off-season? "That's—" I start. "Whoa."

"*Ha-haaa!*" Santa drags out the last half of his laugh. "What's your name, my friend?"

"Tretch—or, well, Richard. Richard Farm the Third."

"It's nice to meet you, Richard Farm the Third. You like to travel?"

"Well." I tip my head to the side, trying to think. Where have I ever even been outside of Warmouth, other than Farm Farm? "Yeah, I guess I like to travel."

Santa lifts his mug and takes a swig. "Excellent. Seems natural if you like to read. Reading's just another form of travel, after all."

"Do you hitchhike alone?"

"For the most part. But I don't mind. My son did one with me a while back, but he's grown now, got a wife and kids. My own wife passed about ten years ago. She and I used to go."

Santa looks reflective for a minute, like he's remembering something really specific. It isn't until I say "I'm sorry" that he snaps back.

"*Sorry?* Heavens, boy, whatever *for?*"

"Your, uh—" I gulp. "Your wife, I mean."

"Oh. Well, you know how it goes." He's silent again for a moment. "You might think it's a sad story—a grieving widower who had to hit the road and hitchhike all across the country to escape his pain, but I'm telling you, Mr. Farm, that is not the case." He leans in. "You know, all the love my wife gave me during this lifetime stayed right where she put it. Even after she was gone. It stayed right here with me, and I *feel* it, alive as all get-out, *every single day.*"

I think about that. In a way it seems exactly like what everyone always tells you. But somehow it feels different coming from the Jim Cho's Santa Claus.

"You'll find that to live is to gather the good things, Mr. Farm," he tells me. "If it's love, you gather it. If it's memory, you gather it. And then when you go, what you'll leave behind you everywhere is . . ."

He holds out his hand for me to finish the thought.

"Uhh . . . more good things?" I try.

"You got it! That's it exactly! *Right-o*, my boy!" He snaps his fingers and drains the rest of his coffee.

The little chime above the door sounds again. A man steps into Mabel's, rubbing his hands. He doesn't look *quite* as scraggly as the Jim Cho's Santa. He's missing the long white beard, but I figure they're probably around the same age. He stands at the door.

"Hey, Quaker!" the man shouts. "You ready to go?"

"Whoops," Santa says, standing. "I think I let the time get away from me, Mr. Farm." He reaches into his pocket. "Hold on, let me pay this girl," he calls out to the guy who's just come in.

Amy steps from behind the counter. The man stands in the doorway and yanks on a pair of gloves, mumbling something about a "big waste of money" and "not even keeping anything warm."

Santa looks at me. "He's just mad because I made him buy a pair of gloves before we left town." He tips some change onto the table from his tattered wallet and places a single dollar bill on top.

"Well, Mr. Farm." He reaches for my hand again, and we shake. "It was a pleasure talking to you."

"You, too, uh, 'Quaker'?"

He nods. "Yes, that's my travel name, or *trail* name, if you prefer."

I shake his hand, and then, because I don't know what to say next, tell him, "Well, enjoy your adventure."

That's when he smiles.

"You, too, Mr. Farm."

He lets go of my hand and walks to the door, his friend still fussing about the gloves. "Woulda been perfectly fine without 'em," he's saying. Then the door swings shut, sounding the chime again.

Amy comes to clear the table. "Who was *that*?" she asks.

"That was the Jim Cho's Santa Claus," I tell her.

I open my copy of *On the Road* to page one. *I first met Dean not long after my wife and I split up.* Amy scoops the change into her hand and counts.

"Well, he only tipped a nickel."

I look up. "I'll tip you good, Amy. Don't worry."

She smiles. "Tretch, you are the nicest guy. Anyone ever tell you that?"

I shrug.

"Well, you *are*," she says. "You really, really are."

She carries the money and Santa's mug behind the counter before returning to fill my mug. I sit reading until dark.

Neither of us mentions Matt.

nineteen

I don't hear from Matt again until New Year's Eve Eve. By that point, there have been three silent days between us.

"Tretch!" Mom calls. "Phone's for you!"

I know it's him. I feel weird—so naturally I act it, too.

"Huh-lo," I whisper-croak into the phone.

"Wow, Tretch, that was the gloomiest 'hello' you could have offered. What's up? All good?"

"Oh, yeah, yeah," I say, still weakly.

"Oh, okay . . . Well, I'm home now, and I was calling about the dance tomorrow. Do you want to pick Lana up first or me first?"

"Uh, I don't really care. Does it matter to you?"

"*Weeellll*, maybe you can pick Lana up first? That way, you guys can have some nice private time before I show up."

I don't know how to convey to him that it *really* does not matter to me. I think I've voiced my agreement/ambivalence, but apparently I haven't said anything.

"Tretch? You still there?"

The line goes quiet. I flash back to his phone call over the holidays. The spotty service. I hold my breath for a second, leaving the line silent. Maybe this is revenge. I don't know.

"Tretch? Hel-*lo*?"

"I'm here, I'm here. Sorry, service is a little spotty inside my house." *Lie.*

"Oh, okay. So you pick up Lana first? Around nine since the party starts at nine, but we don't want to be the first ones there, obviously."

"Yep, that sounds good. I'll let Lana know."

"Okay, great! I am so excited. This is going to be awesome! And I can spend the night afterward?"

"Indeed," I respond. I say it quickly, like a robot with no sense of voice inflection patterns.

"You okay, Tretch-o? You sound a little off, buddy."

"Yeah, yeah, *yeah*." I doth protest a little too much, perhaps—"I'm fine, dude"—but of course Matt doesn't notice.

"Oh, okay," he says. "Just checking."

"Yeah, maybe I'm just a little nervous, is all."

Lie.

I'm not really nervous at all. In fact, I'm the opposite of nervous. I'm kind of numb. I kind of don't care about any of this. I'm quiet in the car on the way to pick up Lana, and Mom asks, "You're not getting sick again, are you?"

I say, "No, but I don't feel very good."

I pinch the scarf in between my knees. I'd put it on earlier when I was getting ready. But I snatched it off as soon as I got in the car. I think it looks dumb on me.

Mom drums the steering wheel with her thumb. "Well, maybe a little social interaction will be nice? I can't believe you haven't asked Matt to come over the last couple days. Hasn't he been home since—"

"Mom, sometimes I just like to be quiet."

"Oh." She clams up suddenly like she's scared or something, like I've intimidated her. God, I feel like I'm going to cry. I feel like the king of the screwups. I didn't mean it as in *Mom, stop talking. I want to be quiet right now.* I meant it as, like *Mom, sometimes I don't want to be social or have interactions. Sometimes I don't* want *Matt to come over.* But when I start to explain, Mom interrupts, "Oh, no, let's be quiet by all means. Start this new year off right."

The rest of the car ride, she's straight-faced, and I feel bad.

We don't say a word. We don't even turn on the radio. When we get to Lana's house, a brick-walled one-story with a light blue door, I hop out. "Okay, I'll be right back," I say, but Lana's already opened up the blue door, closed it, and begun to advance toward the car.

"Uh, hi," I say.

" '*Uh, hi,*' " she mimics, smiling.

"Lana, you remember my mom," I say. "She was with me that day at Books—not to bring up a sore matter . . ."

I'm talking about our Gatsby argument, not that she lost her job. But when Lana responds, "Oh, Tretch, it's not a sore matter. I couldn't care less," I realize it wasn't clear. She opens the back door to the car and gets in. "Hi, Mrs. Farm! Remember me?"

"Hi, Lana," Mom says, a big smile now. "Yes, of course I remember you. How are you?"

"I'm doing very well, thanks."

When we show up at Matt's a little after nine, I don't get out of the front seat. A few seconds pass and Mom suggests I go knock on the door, when he appears. He's holding a vegetable platter.

"Tretch, were you supposed to bring a refreshment?" Mom asks, her voice all panic-charged.

"No, it's fine," I say.

"Do you want to come hop in the back with me?" Lana asks.

"No, it's fine."

The truth of the matter is, I was feeling pretty numb, but not numb enough to be oblivious to the fact that it's a jerky thing to do, to not go sit with her in the back. She's never spoken a direct word to Matt in her life.

Oh, well, I figure. *At least Lana's not shy or anything.*

"What's up, every*one*?" Matt says as he sets the vegetable platter on the seat between him and Lana. Mom says, "Hi, Matt." Lana says, "Hi."

I allow my head a half turn. "What's up?" I reply, and there's a beat afterward, during which Mom reaches for the radio dial and turns it on. "I just don't understand these stations that play Christmas music after Christmas is over. You want to find something?" She directs the question at me.

"Sure," I say, pleased because now I have an excuse to spend a small portion of the ride focused on the radio and nothing else. When I settle on a station, I busy myself by stuffing Grandma's scarf into my pocket. Matt and Lana talk politely in the backseat.

Or, rather, Matt talks, and I guess it's politely.

"Your first dance, too?"

I catch Lana's wide-eyed face in the rearview. "Oh, uh—" she starts as Mom takes a left onto Barrow. "Yeah, I guess I'm just not much of a dancer."

"Well, you picked a good date, then. Didn't she, Tretch?"

I reply quickly. "Yep."

It's the only word I share until we arrive.

· ·

Sinks's Young-'n-Fit is a big building with cement walls on the outside. It has no windows, just a back door with a fire escape and two big double doors on the front.

Mom pulls the Accord into the parking lot. "Y'all want me to go in with—?"

"Mom, *no*."

"I was just kidding, Tretch. Geez." She brakes, and we all unbuckle. "Have *fuuun*!" She's trying to be funny now. "I love you, Tretch, my little man. I hope you have so much fun . . ." She makes kissy noises.

"Mom, *stop*." I slide out of the passenger seat and slam the door. When she rolls down the window, I try giving her the *go away* look, but she either doesn't get it or she simply ignores it. "Tretch, I'm just messing with you. You know I have to mess with you. You three have a blast. I'll be back to pick y'all up."

I nod. "Thanks, Mom."

"Love you, Tretch."

"I love you, too, Mom."

She rolls up the window and, soon enough, the Accord is moving out of the parking lot. For a split second there, I really do wish I could just go with her, do something fun and lame instead for New Year's Eve, like we did last year—playing Monopoly (in hopes of good fortune!) and watching the ball drop on TV.

Matt holds his veggie tray proudly, like it's his ticket into the dance. Lana presses into my arm with her shoulder. She's nervous, I can tell. It makes sense, really. She's a little out-there, after all.

She grabs my arm. "Tretch," she says. "Wait."

Matt stops at the double doors and turns. "Y'all coming?"

"Uh . . ." I turn to Lana. "One second, Matt."

He hesitates, holding on to the door handle. I look at Lana and see the panic crossing her face.

"Go on ahead," I say to him. "We'll be a sec."

He winks. And I think, *Honestly? What does he think I'm about to do? Kiss her?* He pushes open the door with his back. Some bass-heavy rap music spills out through the crack, and he disappears. I wonder if I'll see him again for the rest of the dance.

"I—I don't want to go," Lana stammers. "I don't want to go in there."

"But," I say. "We *have* to. We're already *here*."

"Tretch, I just . . ." She looks down. I catch a tiny scuff mark on the top of her white flat. "Everyone . . . everyone's gonna be in there, and . . ."

"And *what*? Amy's there. She's your *friend*, Lana."

"I don't *have* any friends, Tretch! I don't . . . I don't really *know* anyone, and nobody even *tries* to know me." She tugs at the edges of her skirt. "I mean, what am I *wearing*?" She looks up at me frantically for an explanation.

"Lana, you look nice," I say. "You look very nice."

That's when she starts to sob.

"Oh, *yeah*?" she says. "Well, if I look so nice, then how come—" Her nostrils flare like a bull's in a cartoon. "How come you didn't sit in the backseat with me on the way here?"

"What?"

"How come you don't like me, Tretch?"

"Lana, I—"

"I mean, is it because my family's Jewish and you guys are Christian? 'Cuz if it is . . ."

"*Lana.*" I place a hand on her shoulder. "Lana, why on *earth* would that be it?"

"That was Andy McRae's reason!" She turns her face and wipes her nose. "That's what he said when I gave him a valentine in the seventh grade."

"In the seventh grade? Lana, you're in *high school* now."

"It's just the same, Tretch." She shakes her head. "Everyone says it's different and that everyone acts more grown up and stuff like that, but it's not true. It's really just the same." She wipes her face with the back of her hand and pushes one big breath through her mouth—"*Hoooo*"—like it's the relief she needs.

"And, Tretch, you don't have to like me. I just . . . I really like that you like books and that you're smart and that you dress nice and . . ." She looks into my eyes. *Oh no*, I think. *Here it comes.* Somehow I'm prepared even though it's never happened before.

Lana's face and puckered lips swoop in fast. There's no time to even think about dodging. "Lana—" I start, but she lands it.

My first kiss.

Quick as it happens, it's over.

"—I'm gay."

Lana pulls back. "What?" The expression on her face isn't quite shock. It's something else.

"I—I—" Now it's my turn to stammer. "I, yeah, well, like I said . . ."

"Oh." She's quiet for a moment, observing me. "Really?"

I nod.

"Well," she tries, "I guess that explains your *Great Gatsby* theory, then?"

I laugh nervously. "Yeah. You could say my gaydar is pretty fine-tuned, and Nick Carraway totally gives me the red alert."

She tries to smile, not successfully. "Am I the last one to know? I mean, does everyone else know? How stupid am I right now?"

"Nobody knows," I confess. "I mean, my brother knows. But nobody else. So you're not stupid at all. Really."

"Oh," she says, taking in all this information. Strangely, I'm not worried that she knows. Well, not any more than a little bit.

"So," she says, "I guess this changes things a little bit, doesn't it?" She laughs through the last part, a smile appearing.

But I have to challenge her. "What does it change?" I ask, staring at her fiercely. "Tell me."

"Uhh . . . It means, well, obviously, we could never date."

"Oh yeah, *that*," I say. "But, really, what does it *change*?"

Lana raises an eyebrow. "Uhhh . . ."

"*Nothing!*" I answer for her. "It changes absolutely *nothing*. Isn't that great? I am still Tretch Farm, and you are still Lana Kramer, and we are still two Warmouth misfits standing outside of what is destined to be a god-awful first high school party experience for both of us. *But,* more importantly, you like me for being me, and I like you for being you, and you know what that says to me, Lana Kramer?"

She shakes her head.

"It says to me that we are friends."

Just then, a white Jeep pulls in, and we face each other. I turn to my side and hold out my arm for her to take. "But don't think for a moment," I say, "that if I *were* straight, I wouldn't try to lasso the moon for you." Her face goes pink. "You're worth the moon, Lana Kramer. And then some."

She smiles and, looking down, says softly, "We both are."

I can trust her. I know I can trust her. My secret is safe with her. And, even better, it doesn't feel like it needs to be a secret. Not with her.

Does she understand all this? I'm not sure.

All I'm sure of is that she takes my arm, and together we push through the double doors, Katy Perry's "Teenage Dream" pounding down the darkened hallway. *This is it*, I think. *This is the teenage dream.* We turn a corner and behold the dance floor.

Totally unoccupied.

I lean into Lana and whisper, "Isn't this supposed to be a dance party?"

People line the walls, just waiting for someone to make the first move. I even see Matt pulling the plastic top off of his veggie plate and lifting up a celery stick to take a bite. Amy is standing next to him.

I take a step back from Lana and grip her hand. She lifts her chin.

"After you," I say, gesturing with my free hand.

"Oh, Tretch, *no*—" she starts, but I spin her out anyway. Lana's words—*"We both are"*—echo in my head as she twirls. "Well, I suppose if you *insist*," she says when she comes to a stop, her face all red and smiley. "Woo! I'm dizzy now!" She's laughing—not an embarrassed laugh, either, but a real one.

"I'm not nervous about all these people watching—are you, Lana Kramer?"

"Let them watch, Tretch Farm."

"Just checking," I say, and as if on cue, the chorus hits. *"We both are!"* I cry, and it's like I'm going into battle, which I'm not—or maybe I am, symbolically? A battle to save this party? Lana's doing these spectacular arm movements, flailing them out to either side of her and bringing them up in a peak above her head, cupping her hands. It's like she's crowning herself. Her eyes are closed, and I get it. Dancing is spiritual. Dancing is personal. Some people look at a dancing person and say, *What a total show-off.* They only notice the body of the dancing person. They look at the way the elbows jut out, the way the hips shake and the neck bends. They criticize all of these things, saying, *This dancing person shouldn't be dancing. This dancing person has no rhythm!*

But the dancer is immune to all of this.

"Hey, Tretch," someone behind me says.

I spin around. "Oh, *hey*, Amy!"

"I'm pretty sure I've told you this before," she says, pressing her hip to mine, "but you're magic, you know that?"

Amy pirouettes away, her fingers fluttering, and I swear that girl is half bird the way she flies. She flies into Matt's arms, of course, and I look away. A few couples are out on the floor now, and I'm spinning across it in search of Lana.

I can't help it, though. I look back again. Matt and Amy are bobbing in place on the floor, and I get the sense that Amy wishes Matt were a better dancer, even though he really is going for it. His eyes are shut. His head is nodding. He's feeling it. It's awesome.

Good, I think. *Good for you, Matt.* I spin around again and see Lana. On either side of her are two people, Anna

McCreigh and Paul Goodroe, and I can tell that Lana has danced herself unknowingly in between them. I can't help but smile. I am not out of breath, but my throat is dry.

"Hey, Lana!" I call.

Her back is to me. Her arms go up as the final chorus hits. She crowns herself again.

"Lana!" I make my way over to her as Paul and Anna hop aside, fist-pumping like most of the other dancers on the floor.

She turns around. "Oh, hi, Tretch," she says, smiling. "This is the best."

"Yeah, it totally is. Um, do you want to get some water?"

"Sure." She smiles as we join the fist-pumping masses, hopping until we safely reach the double doors.

"I think we got it started, Lana," I say as we exit into the dark hallway of Sinks's Young-'n-Fit. If this were a scene from a TV show and Lana and I were your typical teenage couple at a New Year's dance, then maybe we would swing a couple dance moves by ourselves, right there in the dim hallway. Then a slow song would start playing and we'd hold each other close and sway.

But instead Lana goes for the water fountain and comes up wiping sweat from her forehead. "Whoo!" she says. "You're right, that was something else! I never knew you could dance like that!"

"Well, I've had a lot of practice." I take my turn at the fountain and slurp.

A slow song comes on. I gulp my water back. "Oh no." It's that song "Desperado" by the Eagles. And no disrespect to them. I love the Eagles. There was a solid month last year where Joe played the *Hotel California* album on repeat in his car. But this song? At a New Year's dance party?

Lana's eyes get big, and a smile spreads across her face. "What is *this*?"

"He's totally gonna kill what we started," I say. "In one song, that DJ is going to murder it." We don't say anything for a moment. Her eyes dart to the corner of the hallway and then back up at me. I take another swig of water from the fountain—

"So are you in love with him?" she asks.

—and start choking.

"*What?*" I muster when I come up for air, pounding my chest. "*Who?*"

"Come on. You know who."

"Veggie tray?"

"Exactly."

I look at Lana. I know I can be honest with her. She isn't one of those conniving types. Sure, she stole some books from her cousin's bookstore and got fired, but who cares about that?

"Yes," I tell her. "I think I am."

Lana nods. "Wow. That kills me."

"What do you mean?"

"It's just so . . . *sad*."

"Hey," I say. "I don't know about you, but I'm great."

"Tretch!" Lana smiles. "You are—"

"What?"

"A total freakin' hero, dude."

I do a kind of mock dance to the twangy sound coming from the dance floor. "So, is it just me or is this song almost over?" I wink and grab Lana by the hand. "Come on. Let's put in a request with the DJ. We'll really be heroes if we can save this dance."

She follows me back down the hallway and across the dance floor. Again, everyone is standing on the sides of the gym like giraffes at a watering hole. The DJ sits on the far side of the floor, behind a big table with all his equipment spread out on it. He is big, with long hair and a beard and sunglasses with headphones on. I watch him typing stuff into a small silver laptop and wonder what fresh cut of our parents' favorite tunes he has planned for us next. Can't he see that no one's having any fun?

"Hey," I say.

He pulls an ear of his headphones away from his head. "What up, kid?"

"You got any Ellie Goulding?" I ask. "That song 'Anything Could Happen'?"

"Sure, I got that. You wanna hear it?"

"You got it, boss," I say. I figure since he called me "kid," I can call him "boss."

"Let me see." He looks at his computer screen. "Got it. Here ya go, kid." He messes around with some buttons on a board on the equipment table, and voilà!

The familiar *eeh-eeh-eeh*s burst through the speakers. They push me forward to the middle of the dance floor. (I swear, those *eeh*s have a mind of their own, and that beat! It's magical.) I feel like Dean Moriarty from *On the Road*. I feel like he feels whenever he hears good jazz. It's like everything is shouting at me, "Go! Tretch! Go! Go!" and, before I know it, I am bobbing up and down, flapping my arms, working the moves I've practiced at home. And to think, all that time I spent at home preparing, never knowing that this moment was the reason why. This moment. And nothing else. There is only space in my head for two things: the music and my moves.

I forget to bring Lana onto the dance floor with me. This time, I am on my own. I cock my hip to the side and pull the scarf from my pocket. I hold it high above my head. The steady beat of the first verse is climbing, has been climbing now for a while, almost there, almost to the peak, the chorus, *"anything could happen, anything could happen,"* and then it hits.

The beat does more than spark.

It explodes.

I look up at the ceiling with my head tipped back and my neck stretched out, shaking my shoulders and waving my arms. I look down at the ground and shake my elbows, my hips. I'm looking everywhere while I move, everywhere but right at

Matt Gooby. *Don't look at him.* The thought comes clearly. *Forget about him.* I move like crazy, harder than I've ever moved, and I am sweating. I feel it on my forehead and inside my shirt. I feel it down the legs of my pants. For one quick portion of the dance, I am on the ground doing a roll-around, and when I pop up, some dust sticks to my arms. The floor hasn't been swept, which helps when I move into the moon-walk (I've only ever accomplished this before in socks), which draws applause.

I hear calls of *"Go, Tretch!"* and *"Do it, boy!"* But that doesn't matter. I'm not dancing for them.

The song is almost over—just a few more steps.

"Anything could happen, anything could happen."

I focus on them and give them my all.

"Eeh, eeh, eeh, eeeeh."

I punch my fists through the colored light coming from the spotlights.

"Eeh, eeh, eeh, eeeeh."

I hop. *It's almost over, it's almost over,* I tell myself. I look left, I look right, the last line of the song comes, and Matt's face appears in front of me. *"But I don't think I need you"*— and then it's over.

"Tretch! Tretch!" He's shouting and shaking my shoulders. "That was *incredible!* I never knew y—"

I reach back for him, but I'm getting swept away by everyone around us. Hands pull me by my arms and shoulders into the heated crowd. Everyone is chanting, "*Tretch. Tretch. Tretch. Tretch.*" It feels like a good dream.

I feel brave like I never have before, and I think everyone else feels it, too. Because by the next song, there's not a soul who isn't dancing. It's all of us, all of us together, and I'm telling you, it's miraculous.

twenty

After the party, we find Mom parked outside Sinks's Young-
'n-Fit. We're all beat and happy, and as I step off the curb into
the parking lot, I swear I could fly.

It's like Mom can tell. "*So?*" she asks, all excited. "How
was it?"

Matt speaks up immediately. "Oh man, Mrs. Farm, it was
great. Did you know Tretch could *move* like he can? *Gah—*"

"Really?" Mom eyes me as I get into the passenger seat.
"You got the moves, then, huh, Tretch?"

"He really does, Mrs. Farm," Lana chimes in. She's beaming, her face still flushed.

"Well, *all right*." Mom slaps me five. "Go, Tretch."

"Yeah, it was fun," I say. "We had a lot of fun."

We drive Lana to her house and drop her off. She slides out of the backseat. "See ya, Tretch," she says. "Swing by Mabel's sometime." Then, like she's just remembered he was there, too, she adds, "You, too, Matt."

"Will do, Lana."

"Will do."

Mom waves out the window as we drive off. *"Happy New Year, Lana!"* She turns to us. "I *like* that girl. She's such a sweetie."

"See, Tretch? What did I tell ya?" Matt says from the backseat. He pokes me in the shoulder.

"She's a good friend," I say. I turn in my seat to face Matt. "Just a good friend. And I honestly don't want it any other way."

"Maybe not for *now*," Matt prods.

"Or maybe not *forever*." I say this a little more forcefully than I intended. Matt slumps back against the seat.

"Tretch," Mom says in her *Things okay?* voice.

"I mean, *agh*, I'm sorry. That sounded bad, sorry." I turn my head to the window. A graveyard flies by in the night, and I'm just like, *What have I done? The first good night since Christmas, and I'm ruining it.* "I mean, it's nothing against Lana at all. It's just, it's *me*, really—"

"What do you mean?" Matt asks. "You two like all the same things."

That's it, I decide. I've had it with the whole "you like the same things" argument. I turn in my seat. "Matt, it is *possible* to like *different* things and still fall in love, you know?"

"I—"

"In fact, some people argue that when two people who like *different* things fall in love, it brings all kinds of new and exciting things to the table. For both of them!"

"Yeah, yeah, I know," Matt says. "I didn't mean . . ."

"Tretch," Mom says, this time in her *What's gotten into you?* voice. And honestly, what *has* gotten into me? I'm being a jerk to Matt.

"I'm sorry to be pushy. I know it's annoying."

It is annoying!

"I just want you to . . ." he starts.

What? He just wants me to . . . what?

"Never mind," he finishes.

"What?" I press him. I want to know.

"I just want you to have someone. You know, like, after I leave Warmouth. But, I mean, if you and Lana are just going to be friends, that's fine, too. As long as you have someone when I leave. Friend, girlfriend, whatever, it really doesn't matter to me. As long as you're not alone."

What black magic hath Ellie Goulding wrought this night?

This is not the Matt Gooby I know. This is not *my* best friend. This is an *actual* best friend. This is him saying, *I care about you, Tretch Farm, and I'll still care about you even after I'm gone.*

"You care so much for other people," he continues. "But I worry that, after I'm gone, there won't be anyone at school to care for *you.*"

I am looking out my window. I don't want to see the expression on Mom's face as Matt says these things, and I really don't want her to see mine. I don't want her to see it as it sinks in, as I realize, Matt *does* love me.

He *loves* me, and he only knows the half of me, the half I let him see. The same goes for Mom, for Dad, for Grandma and Granddad. For everyone, really, except for Joe and Lana. This whole time I've been picturing my secret as something I've been keeping to protect them, to make it easier for them to love me. But instead I've just been robbing them—robbing them of the chance to love the full me.

I've been making it harder on them.

"Hmm," I say. "Well, don't worry about me, Matt. I'll be—" I realize now that I have to tell him. "I'll be fine. Really. I mean, I'll miss you and all, don't get me wrong."

"I'm gonna miss you, too, Tretch," he says. "My best friend."

I turn in my seat to look at him. Mom has been quiet all this time, which I appreciate. Her eyes are straight ahead on the road. *I have to tell them all*, I think. *But when?*

"Matt," I say. "In case you ever had any doubt, you are my best friend, too. And everyone knows, you never meet anyone in your whole life who means exactly the same thing to you that your first best friend means. It just doesn't work that way."

I turn back around in my seat.

"You must have read that somewhere," he says, laughing.

Once we get back to my house and my room, Matt starts doing that thing where he takes off all his clothes in front of me before he gets in the shower. He's still talking about the dance. "I mean, *Tretch*, you gotta teach me those moves. Did you see how everyone was crowding around you? Total genius, dude."

"Matt," I say. He's unbuckling his belt, and I think, *Well, now's as good a time as any.* "I'm gay," I say. "Uh, sorry it took so long for me to tell you."

Matt's elbows sag at his sides, his hands still gripping his belt buckle. The look on his face is so warm, I think for a moment he might be about to confess, too.

So this is it, I think. *If it's ever going to happen, it's going to happen now, and he'll tell me that he's gay, too, and that all his girl-craziness talk has just been his cover-up, because, like me, he was just too embarrassed to say anything before.*

"Tretch," he says. "That's awesome. I mean, you know it's cool with me and all, since I *am* the one with two gay dads here, but—" He smiles. "Thanks for telling me."

I bob my head. "You're welcome."

I want to leave the room before Matt drops his pants. Honestly, I'm not even sure if he *will* drop his pants now that I've told him. That would just be disrespectful, right? Or maybe it would be disrespectful for him *not to*, since he normally would? I don't know.

"I'm going to run and grab a sleeping bag downstairs for me to sleep in. Oh, and maybe when you get out, we'll go downstairs and watch the ball drop on TV."

"Sweet deal," he says.

I turn to leave.

"Oh, and, Tretch—"

"Yeah?" My hand is on the doorknob.

"I mean, *really*, thanks, uh—" He hesitates. "Uh, thanks for telling me. I know it's . . . Well, I know it's not the easiest thing. It's a big deal."

"Aww, psh." I shake my head. He'll never know how right he is. "It was a lot easier than I was making it out to be. Trust me."

He laughs. "Attaboy."

Downstairs, in the living room closet, I'm about to exhume— from beneath a hoard of wrapping paper and Mom's arts and crafts supplies—Joe's old sleeping bag from elementary school, when I start to really think about what I'm doing.

Before tonight, Matt and I would have slept in the same bed together, no questions asked. But now that I've come out to him and all, here I am in a closet scrounging around for a sleeping bag so we don't have to.

Matt didn't ask me to do this.

Is there a reason why I'm doing this?

Possible answers:

A) No. Nothing has really changed; you are the same devoted friend, good sheets-sharer, light sleep-tosser you were *before* you came out to him.

B) Yes. Nothing has really changed; *you are still in love with him, for crying out loud!* And to sleep in the same bed as him would only incite misguided imaginings and instill hard-to-dislodge hopes in you that one day, someday, maybe . . . this kind of thing could be for real.

C) No. Something *has* changed; you are not in love with him anymore. So, go ahead, sleep with him!

C) Really, Tretch. Think about it . . .

C) At the dance party, *okay?* Remember that part in the song, during the chorus, when Ellie

shouts, *"But I don't think I need you!"* You
looked straight at him! It was like those words
were yours, man!

C) I don't know, Tretch. Maybe don't listen to me.
Are you still in love with him? If so, I'd suggest
answer B, or possibly A.

D) No. There is no reason you should feel like
you can't sleep in the same bed as your friend,
Tretch. Don't be ridiculous.

C) *Oh!* And one more thing! What did it feel like,
Tretch? When you heard the words, *"But I don't
think I need you!"* What did it feel like? Did it
feel like you had just let go of a balloon you'd
been holding on to for so long you were about to
just give up and let it drag you up, up, and away,
until you either (A) asphyxiated, (B) disintegrated
in the atmosphere, or (C) both A and B? *Or!
Maybe!* Did it feel the way you feel, like when
you let go of a sleeping bag—one that you've
loaded down with *all* of this extra meaning—
and watch it fall to the closet floor . . . but
maybe minus that satisfying thud sound?

Is that what it felt like, Tretch? Is that what it felt like?
I love Matt. I know I do.

But the thing is, for the first time, it feels kind of like our loves are . . . the *same*. And one love is not stronger or deeper or more hopeless or more honest.

Am I still in love with Matt Gooby?

Maybe. But what I feel now is different.

I feel it without the hurt.

Upstairs, Joe is brushing his teeth in the hallway bathroom. The hum of the electric toothbrush reminds me of Granddad, of his current welding project, the angel wings. Maybe he's managed to make some real progress in the last few days without me barging in on him inside his shop all the time.

"Hey, Joe." I stick my head around the corner of the bathroom door. Joe's already in his pajama attire—plaid bottoms with a Ramones T-shirt. "Happy New Year," I say.

"*Happy New Year, Mr. Potter!*" he replies, his mouth making funny shapes around the toothbrush. He takes a handful of sink water from the tap, and the toothbrush buzzing stops.

"You have a good night?" I ask.

Joe spits. "Yeah, except for I ate, like, ten slices of pizza . . ."

"*Oof.*"

"Yeah." Joe dries his face on the hand towel by the sink. "But it was nice to bring in the new year with Melissa and a few of her friends. Pretty low-key. Melissa's friend Becky

Ambrose reads tarot cards, so she read all of ours out loud for us. And you want to know what my *first* card was?"

"Yeah."

"The Death card. I almost had a panic attack. But Becky said that it doesn't mean like actual, *literal* death. It just means like change, shirking off something old and sinking into something new."

"Oh," I say. "Interesting."

"Yeah! So I really think it was just talking about college and me moving away and stuff, but at first, when I saw it was the Death card, I was like . . ."

"Granddad?" I ask.

"Exactly! So you thought it, too."

"Initially, yeah."

Joe shrugs. "I guess we sort of know what our greatest fear of the moment is." He turns from the mirror to me. "How was your night?"

"Good," I say. "I, uh, I came out to a couple people."

"Wow, that's . . . At the dance? Who?"

"Matt and Lana. Matt after the dance. He's here now."

Joe leans his hip against the sink. "That's awesome." He crosses his arms, smiles. "It go okay?"

I nod.

"What made you decide to do it? Just a sudden upsurge of bravery?"

I laugh. Maybe it was the dance? The feeling of all those

hands beneath me, lifting me up. I tell Joe, "I don't know, exactly. I mean, if you can't come out to your best friend on New Year's Eve, then when can you?"

Joe's smile cracks open. "Hmm. New year, new leaf. I still say it takes some bravery, Tretch-o. Who knows? This coming year might just be the bravest year of your life."

"Yours, too," I say. "With college."

"Yeah, maybe. I guess we'll see, won't we?"

"Yeah, I guess." I notice myself in the mirror. Funny, I hadn't even realized I was smiling before, but now I see it. It's not all that big or anything, but it's there, effortlessly, honestly. "I guess we'll see."

When I walk into my room, Matt doesn't search for the sleeping bag on me. In fact, he doesn't search for anything at all. The lights are out, and he's stretched across my bed, his hair wet from the shower, in a peach-colored T-shirt and plaid pajama pants from my closet. His eyes are closed.

"Matt?" I ask.

Then they flutter open. "Hmm?"

"You asleep already?"

"What? Uhh, no, no—" He struggles to sit up. "I just, uh, geez, please tell me it's not morning already."

"Ha! No, no. Oh my God, you were actually asleep. That was like the quickest falling-asleep I've ever seen . . ."

"What can I say? We went hard on the dance floor tonight."

"True dat."

Matt's hands flop into his lap and he smiles. I can see his eyes blinking in the dark, and when he smiles—I can see that, too. "Happy New Year, Tretch."

"Happy New Year, Matt. Now, scooch over so I can have some room."

twenty-one

At 4:30 a.m., the phone rings. Matt is sleeping on his stomach, with his hands between his hips and the mattress. His face is tilted to the side, and his mouth hangs open. Several long, slow breaths escape. He stays sound asleep—even through the sound of the screaming telephone.

Finally, I hear Dad answer it. "Hello?" he says. But the rest I can't make out. I slide out of the bed, open the bedroom door, and walk downstairs.

The lights in the kitchen are on. Dad's brewing a pot of coffee, his eyelids all puffy.

"What's up?" I ask.

"Mary," Dad tells me. "A little later than expected, but she's finally having that calf."

"Oh," I say. "Is it—?"

"It's a breech."

"Uh-oh."

"Better go wake Joe."

"Okay." I start out of the kitchen.

"You think you'll be able to help us?"

I turn. "Oh, yeah, sure," I say, even though the last time this happened it was nothing short of traumatic. "But if we're all going to go, I better wake Matt, too."

"Well." Dad nods. "If nothing else, it'll be a new experience for him, I guess."

"Yeah," I say, and turn to go up the stairs.

The Farm Farm house is lit up when we get there. Grandma has made biscuits already, and they sit on a warm baking sheet, butter melting out from the center of each one. Granddad is pacing the living room.

"Better get them biscuits to go," he says. He looks Matt up and down but doesn't introduce himself. I think Matt is still too tired to notice, though. Grandma pushes two biscuits into his hands, two into mine, and two into Joe's.

"Thanks, Grandma," I say.

"No trouble." Grandma waves her hand. "I knew y'all

wouldn't have had time to eat anything." The clock on the microwave says it's now 5:37.

"Y'all *ready*?" An anxious hum carries Granddad's voice. "I cain't *find* her. I found her a little while ago, and now I cain't. Reckon she got scared."

"Is the calf showing at all?" Dad asks.

"Yeah." Granddad gives one nod. "A little bit." His lip curls.

Delivering calves into this world is not Granddad's cup of tea. He gets squeamish at the sight of the birth. Not to mention, it makes him a nervous wreck. The most uptight I've ever seen him was during a breech calf delivery last year. It was the first one I'd ever been around for, and that one had been in the day.

It also hadn't been freezing cold out.

"You think this one's still alive, Grandma?" I ask. The last one was stillborn, and I hadn't been able to look at it.

Grandma shakes her head.

"Joe, run grab the truck," Dad says. "You and Matt drive around and try to find her. Tretch, Granddad, and I will walk around with a lasso—"

Granddad holds up his hand. "Naw, Richard. You better go with them, case they find her. They find her without a lasso, they'll just scare 'er off even worse. I don't want her gettin' more upset. The more she run around scared, the harder it'll be on the calf. Me and Tretch'll go on foot. I'll get us some rope."

I gulp. "Uh, rope?"

"For a lasso." Dad winks. "Don't worry," he whispers. "It'll be fine."

I wonder what Matt is thinking about all of this. Lassos and breech calves. Does he even know the word *breech*?

These are not things he's going to need to know in New York City.

"That's when the calf gets all turned around inside its mom," I explain. "You know how the head's supposed to come out first?"

"Yes," Matt says.

"Well, this way it's like the feet are coming out first. That's why Dad has to try and get his hand all in there to turn it around."

Talking about breech calves always makes me feel a little sick. My hands start to feel sweaty. I stick one of the biscuits in my mouth. Matt is chewing on one, too.

"*All right*, Tretch, come *on*!"

Granddad is already out the back door. I see the rope slung over his shoulder. *Dear God, please do not make me have to use that rope on Mary.* I bite the inside of my lip, swallowing biscuit. "Okay, I'm coming, Granddad!" I call, following him out the back door.

I figure Matt is all right to hang tight with Dad and Joe. Honestly, I wish I could stay behind with him. Odds are, when this stuff happens, breech deliveries and all that, some kind of death happens. Usually, your best hope is that it will just be the calf who dies, not its mother, too. It wears away at Granddad when this stuff happens. Sometimes he loses his cool.

He's ahead of me now, going through the woods. I run to catch up. He hears me coming and snaps, "Don't *run*, Tretch. It'll startle 'er if she's round here."

"Whoops," I say. I slow to a walk.

Granddad steps easily. Dried leaves crunch and sticks pop. Everything is dead quiet and *cold*. It is so cold. I can make out the clouds from Granddad's breath though he's a good distance in front of me. He has a flashlight and is shining it into ditches, behind spots crowded with the thick brush, all spots where he's seen cows lying with their newborns before. It could be a peaceful sight when you just happened upon something like that: a cow lying with her newborn, cleaning it off, the birth having gone smoothly without any help needed from a person.

I keep my eyes peeled, though it's hard to see without a flashlight of my own. For the most part, I feel helpless. I know the trick: trying to catch the glint of the flashlight reflected off the mama cow's eye. That's how you try and find one in the dark.

"Doesn't help that she got a black coat," Granddad says.

We stray off of the trail and push through a clump of thickets. Everything would look bright white from the frost if we were in a clearing with moonlight. But we're covered by a thick canvas of treetops up above, and the moon feels far off. The woods seem bigger and scarier in the dark. More leaves crunch beneath us, and breath clouds up around us like blank word bubbles. We say nothing, and I want to know what Granddad is thinking. I know the inside of his head is buzzing. His fear, his nervousness, and really just his hope. He puts everything on the line for his hope. And if it doesn't work out like he hoped, well, it turns into despair.

His artistic temperament: That was the explanation.

But I don't think it's helped me understand him. It's just getting to know him all the years of my life so far. I know when he wants to be quiet. I know when he wants to cut up. I know that, really, I'm more like him than anyone else in my family.

"Tretch," he breathes. He shines his light against a slope rising before us. "See?"

I look hard, following the light as it spreads out and weakens in the distance. And then, surely, the glint of the eye. It's Mary the cow, and she's standing.

"We gotta get close," Granddad whispers. He crouches. "Hold the light."

I take the flashlight and keep it pointed steadily at her.

Granddad begins a slow shuffle forward. He pulls away when the pants of his coveralls snag on some briars. The bramble plant rattles. I see Mary tense at the sight. She's going to run.

The rope slides in its coil from Granddad's shoulder down his arm. The lassoed end touches the top of his boot before he lifts it. He holds it like a cowboy, then swings a big toss.

It falls flat against Mary's side just as she turns and scampers off. Granddad hollers like he's in pain, and I catch glimpse of something I don't want to see swinging from Mary's backside. I stand, shocked. A second passes, and she's gone.

Granddad rests his hands on his knees and crouches. "Gah-*damn*!" He hollers. When he stands up straight, he mumbles, "Too slow, can't do anything anymore."

He walks back toward me, his arm outstretched for the flashlight.

"It's that cancer, Tretch!" He shouts it. "It's that cancer gettin' to me!"

The lasso bobs on the ground as he tugs it back in. "Maybe *you* can do it!" he says, swinging the rope at me. I catch it and hold it for a moment. "Granddad, I—" I start, but he walks past me.

It's the moment when you give up. The moment when hope feels gone, and all you can think about is your failure.

"Granddad," I say again, but I'm out of earshot now. I want to call for Dad. I want to hop in the truck with Dad and Joe and Matt and drive back home, then wake up like it's going to be a normal New Year's Day. None of this breech calf business.

I catch up to Granddad at the trail. "Wait," I say.

"Maybe Rich'll find 'er. I don't know."

"Maybe so," I say. "She looked like she was headed toward the field. That's where they were headed with the truck, weren't they?"

"I reckon."

"Well, let's walk up that way."

I get him to turn around.

We walk along the trail, out of the woods and into the clearing. It's pretty weird to me. The last time I saw the farmland stretched out before me like this, under the cover of night, I wasn't really myself. And now I'm seeing it again, all the frostiness flaring up under the great white moon. It gives me a sick feeling.

What was I afraid of that night?

Matt, vanishing.

Granddad, vanishing.

Everyone . . .

I hear the quiet rumble of the old pickup idling from across the field. We don't have to climb the slope, then. I won't have to look off in the direction of the frozen lake.

"You hear that, Granddad?"

"Huh?"

"The truck."

We stand still and strain our eyes, and then I see it, the truck's taillights beaming red, two bright spots in the dark. The truck sits pointed in the direction of the woods, the beams from the headlights lost somewhere inside. We begin to cross the pasture, Granddad hoping again, saying, "Reckon he found her."

I'm hoping, too.

I'm hoping Dad has managed to lasso Mary and calm her. I'm hoping he will already have the calf delivered by the time we get there. And I'm hoping the calf won't be dead.

Matt is leaning against the tailgate. He turns as we approach. "Tretch," he says. "I lassoed her. Can you believe it?" His voice is excited, but there's worry written all over his face. Like he can't tell if he's done something wrong.

"Good job," I whisper. "Where are Dad and Joe?"

"They're in the woods." Matt points. "You have to follow the headlights. They're way down in there, I think. They told me to stay put, though. I don't think your dad wanted me seeing, in case—"

"Reckon they got her steadied?" Granddad interrupts, his voice heavy with breath. He places a hand on the tailgate next to Matt.

"I don't know, sir," Matt replies. "Might be. I think Joe was holding on to the rope the last time I saw—"

"Tretch, you better go."

I push past some low branches and make my way into the woods again. I'm scared about what I'll see when I get there. Dad made me turn my head the last time. "Tretch, don't look," he'd said, but I'd heard him pulling then, and I'd known. I think about that. I think about Granddad shouting, "It's that cancer, Tretch!" I don't want to walk any farther. I don't want to see what's coming. It's all too hard. I'll never get out from under it.

I hear my dad's shout through the trees. "Joe, hold her!"

I move quickly. Joe sees me first.

"*Tretch!*" he calls. "Come help me *pull*!" Joe holds tight to the lasso as Mary snaps her neck frantically, stressed, struggling to free herself. She tries to back up, and Joe's feet slide. Dad topples over behind her, and I think, *She'll trample him. She won't mean to, but she will.* I jump for the rope, and when I grab it, I puuuuullllll. Harder than anything, I pull. Harder than I've ever tried to pull anything in my whole life. I pull because I think it might be the only thing that can save Dad, the only thing that can save Mary and the calf, and Granddad. I pull like it's the only thing saving my life, too, and the lives of everyone I know. I pull like it's the only thing keeping us all together.

A burst of frosty air shoots from Mary's nostrils, and she leans forward, resting on her forelegs. Joe and I hold the rope firmly, even though the struggle is over. She isn't fighting

anymore. She's calm. I speak to her. "Attagirl. Just calm down."
She bows her head. I can see the outline of my dad working
behind her.

Like last time, I hear the sound of him pulling.

I close my eyes. *Be alive,* I think. *Be alive.* A hand brushes
against my own and holds fast to the rope. When I open my
eyes, I see it's Granddad. He keeps a steady grip on the rope
between me and Joe. " 'S all right, girl," he says to Mary. "We
gon' make it."

"Oof—" My dad's voice erupts. Then there's a dull thud
against hard ground.

Mary lifts her neck.

"Is it—?" I start to ask.

"Tretch, wait," I hear Joe say. But I have to see. I let go
of the rope and step forward. Behind Mary, Dad lies sprawled,
the calf in his lap perfectly still.

"Oh . . ."

It's slimy and wet, its coat the same color as Mary's. Dark
black, without a single speckle of white.

A wet spot on the ground squishes when I step.

"Tretch," Dad warns again. But I want him to know it's
okay, that I understand about death, and I'm not afraid of it,
because death is a part of life. *And I'm not scared of life, no
way, even though it can be hard, and parts of it are sad. There
are still the good things. There will always be the good things.*

And then it moves. The baby moves.

"Dad!"

The baby's eyes open, and he looks up. He shakes.

"Tretch?" Dad starts to fidget. The calf snaps his head back and forth, and Dad tries his best to steady him. "Here, Tretch!" he says. "Here! We got to—"

Granddad shoves me. *"Clean out its nose!"* I collapse to my knees and bend over the newborn. "Hold *still*!" I shout as I grip the wet snout. Luckily it's over before I have time to really think about it.

I pull my hand away, fingers dripping with nasty clear snot stuff, and I remember what it felt like to pass out. But I keep my cool.

Which is more than I can say for Granddad.

"Hot dog, Tretch!" he yells. "Stuff like this happens and I feel like I could go *forever*! Reckon we'll have to name that one Lucky!"

When we finally get back to the house, Granddad sinks into his easy chair. Moments later, he's snoring. I laugh and eye Matt falling asleep on the living room sofa. The smell of breakfast is coming from the kitchen, but I don't know who's awake to eat it. Dad is falling asleep in the rocking chair, and Joe is sprawled out on the living room floor. I'm not tired, though. I feel really okay, actually. And I think it might be nice to try and catch the sunrise.

It's not every day you get to watch the sun rise on a new year.

So I let myself out the back door and cross the yard. And that's when I see them there, hanging from the big oak tree. The angel wings for Uncle Dennis.

Granddad finished them.

twenty-two

After sleeping through the morning and subsequently partaking in the annual Farm Farm New Year's feast (black-eyed peas, turnip greens, hog jowl, sweet potato casserole, and a pork tenderloin), Matt and I are basically restored, energy-wise.

Now it's four o'clock in the afternoon and we're about to load up the car and head back to town, but Matt wants to see Lucky one last time before we do.

It isn't as cold out now with the afternoon sunshine, but there's still a hint of that frozen bite we felt at six a.m. We peel our eyes for Lucky, but so far we haven't seen so much as one cow.

"When are you gonna tell Amy you're moving back to New York?"

"Oh," Matt said. "I told her already. I told her last night."

The dance, I remember. *Was that really only last night?*

"What'd she say?"

"Oh, not much. I mean, she was sad. But, honestly, you saved it, Tretch. You saved that whole dance, really. The second you started to bust those sick moves, it was like she forgot all about being sad. She just wanted to dance and have a good time. I think she's all right. We never got a chance to really get to know each other, but . . ." Matt shakes his head. "I still couldn't believe those moves, man. I mean, you got the moves!"

The moves.

"You keep saying that like you're surprised or something. You think just because I suck at sports, it means I'd be a sucky dancer, too?" I land a punch on his shoulder, and he hops around acting like I've really hurt him.

"Ooh, Tretch so *strooong*," he says. "Don't even know his own strength."

I smile. "Gosh, I'm gonna miss you," I think. But then I realize it isn't a thought. I've actually said it. I've actually told him.

Matt wraps his arm around my shoulder, and we start up the trail to the house. No sight of Lucky, but that's all right. We'll find Lucky another day. "I'm gonna miss you, too," he says. "I mean, you might be about the only thing I *will* miss. Well, that's not true. I mean, I'm gonna miss stuff like this. I'm gonna miss this winter break, and seeing you dance, and climbing the roof with you and Amy." Then he laughs. "I'm gonna miss you coming out."

I snort. "What?" I don't know what he means. I already came out to him, didn't I?

"You know, like, when you finally tell your parents and stuff."

"Oh." I sigh. "Well . . ."

"I mean, I was the first person you told, right?"

"Well, more like third or fourth, actually . . ."

"Serious? You waited *that* long?" He drops his arm and turns to me. "Why'd you do that? I mean, I should've been easy. We tell each other everything."

And what am I supposed to say?

Matt, the reason I didn't tell you sooner is because I fell in love with you on the day you came to church with my family. We were holding hands during the prayer. And somehow I was afraid that if I told you, you would know, and all the pieces would come sliding into place, and then—

"Because I used to have a crush on you."

And then you'd freak.

Matt stands facing me. He puts his hands in his pockets.

"Seriously?"

I nod. "I mean, I'm over it now, but—" Is that the truth? Last time I checked, the jury was still out. "But, for a while there, yeah. I liked you."

He doesn't say anything, so I go on.

"I mean, you were, like, my *protector*, Matt. You stood up for me and stuff, in front of Bobby Handel, in front of all those jerks—"

"Well, that's what friends do, Tretch."

"I know. I get it now. Like I said, I don't like you that way anymore. It was . . . I mean, it's been a while since—" Now I'm definitely lying, because it definitely hasn't been "a while."

But the truth is, while I stand there looking at him, trying to explain, I don't feel the way for Matt that I used to feel.

"I mean, just being honest," I say. "The crush only lasted for, like, a week—"

"A week?"

"Maybe a month, tops."

He squints. "How long ago was this?"

"Mmm. Eighth grade." *Yesterday.*

"Oh, psh," he says. "That's puppy stuff."

I can't help but laugh. *Totally.*

We start back up the trail through the woods, and Matt cuts up by kicking at the frosty hunk of a fallen tree. He gets a running start and kicks with all his might to see how far it goes. The he chases it down and sends it flying again. "Maybe I should go out for kicker," he says. Then he ducks inside a big hollow oak.

"Matt, there could be bats," I warn, and as I do, he screams, *"Ahhhh!"* A bat flies out from behind him, grazing the top of his head. He falls on the ground with his hand to his chest, like he's having a panic attack, and I crack up. I bend over, put my hands on my knees, and all-out belly laugh for what feels like the longest time. Eventually, Matt can't help it, either. His laughter spouts up in cloudy bursts against the cold air.

"Now, *this*," he says. "*This* is what I'm going to miss."

Before we leave Farm Farm, I have one last thing to do. I have to give Grandma the scarf. After all, it's been almost three weeks.

I fold it up into a square and slide it into the kitchen drawer next to her deck of cards. Later, she calls my dad and tells him that she found it.

"—and Tretch left the sweetest note!" she says.

Of course, I don't know exactly how it all played out. Her finding the scarf, that is. But this is how I picture it.

I picture Grandma opening the kitchen drawer to pull out her deck of cards. I picture her seeing the scarf, lifting it up, finding my note attached, and reading it first.

Here is what it said:

Hey Grandma,

*I ran into Mr. Thumb the other day, and he
gave this to me. He said he had been wearing
it around ever since Mrs. Thumb passed
away. But he said it was time to give it to the
person she made it for. She made it for you,
Grandma. She wanted to say thanks for the
pickled okra. And I don't mean to try and
steal her thunder, Grandma, I really don't.
But I wanted to say thanks, too. For being
the bravest person in the whole wide world.
And everything else.*

I love you.

TRETCH

Then I picture her unfolding the scarf, holding it out in
front of her, and smiling. I imagine her saying something to
my granddad, maybe asking him, "How you feeling tonight,
honey?"

"Pretty good," he responds, emphasizing the "good."

"Well, good," she says. "Reckon we oughta celebrate
tonight?"

Granddad looks up at this. "You mean, you're not all cel-
ebrated out?"

Finally, I picture her shaking her head, smiling.

"No, honey," she replies. "Not by a long shot."

twenty-three

Sometimes, when I love a book, I need to get out to finish it. And I mean, get *out*—like, go someplace where I feel like the ending will be all the more momentous.

It's early evening, the day before the last day of winter break. I have ten pages left in *On the Road*.

Mom and Dad don't usually approve of me going out and wandering the streets when it gets close to dark. But it won't take long. It's only ten pages, after all.

So I don't tell them; I just leave.

And I know where I'm headed, too.

..

The grass in the schoolyard is frosted over. The metal bars on the jungle gym are iced, and it looks like if I touch my tongue to it, I'll be stuck until God knows when. I wonder how cold this winter has been compared to last winter in Warmouth. It hasn't snowed or anything, but there's a constant chill. In years past, it's gotten weirdly warm around Christmastime. One Christmas Eve, I even remember wearing a short-sleeve T-shirt.

I prefer the cold in the wintertime, though; it just feels better that way. More momentous.

I pick a swing and tip it up, letting its collection of frost water drizzle out. The sunlight won't last much longer, and if I want to finish the book here, I need to get started. I crack it open, exhale a cloud of breath, and begin reading.

That's when I smell it.

Cigarette smoke.

I turn my head toward the big oak tree at the corner of the yard. Two benches sit there, angled oddly around the tree's vast roots.

Nobody there. No curl of smoke rising up from anywhere that I can see.

But then I hear from behind me a loud, slick scrape, followed by, "Farm! What are you doing here?"

I turn around. And, there, on his way down from what we called "the big slide" as kids, is Bobby Handel.

"*Bobby?*" I ask. "What are you—?"

"*Hey*, don't ask questions!"

Bobby is crossing the enormous sandbox filled with pea gravel where all the jungle gyms are. He has something balled up inside his fist.

Either that, or he's just making a fist.

He stops about halfway to me and bends down like he's about to puke or something. But he doesn't puke. Instead, he digs out a little hole in the pea gravel, drops something in, then covers it up again.

I put two and two together.

"Are you *smoking* out here, *Bobby*?"

He looks up, his face scrunched up and red—from cold or anger or acne, I'm not sure. "*Farm*. I said *no questions*."

"Are you *stupid*?"

That sets him off. Bobby comes running at me full speed.

I don't know what to do. I don't know if I should try to dodge and run. One thing is for certain, though: I'm not about to try to fight Bobby Handel.

Bobby flings himself full force at me and knocks me off the swing. I manage to cling to *On the Road* as he pulls me down, and I hold it up in front of my face. "Bobby! Bobby!" I shout. "Stop!"

He rears his fist back. "Stupid Farm. Probably gonna run tell your dad and get me in trouble—"

"Bobby, what the *hell*?" I push—I push *hard*. Somehow I manage to get him off of me. He slides onto his butt in the wet grass.

"Jesus, Farm," he says.

I sit up. "What the *hell*, okay?" I drop the copy of *On the Road* into my lap and notice its torn cover.

"Aaaggghhhh!" I roar. "You tore my book!"

Bobby looks aghast. "I—" he starts, but I stop him.

"You tore my *book*, Bobby. And all I wanted was to come here and get some peace and quiet, just like I *always* want, but *no*, God forbid I set foot on school property wanting some peace and quiet when *you're* around!" I throw the book—not *at* Bobby directly, but also kind of at him. It sails over his shoulder and lands with a painful crumpling sound.

"Jesus, Farm," he says again.

"And, I mean, are you *smoking* out here? For Christ's sake! Your mom died from *cancer*. Remember that? When we were five? Do you want *cancer*?"

Bobby wrinkles his face. "Sure!" he says. "Sure I want it!"

"You know, my granddad's got cancer, too, now. And, guess what? *He's probably gonna die from it!* And you know what else? He's *not* a smoker! And neither was my grandma when *she* got cancer, and neither was your mom!"

"So *what*?"

"So, what I'm *saying* is that freaking *cancer* is a real enough *possibility* without you having to freaking *ask* for it."

Bobby jumps at me again. "So *what*, Farm! So *what*?"

I press against his shoulders. "Bobby, *stop*!" I shout. "Get a *grip*!"

He wraps his arms around me and lands a punch to my back, though not hard enough to hurt. In fact, Bobby is softening; I feel it. Eventually, it's like I'm holding on to a big stick of butter. *"Bobby,"* I say, out of breath. I feel him shaking. In that moment, a switch flips. Bobby Handel is crying, and I'm holding him, and maybe it's what I wish I could have done for him when we were five. When he was five years old and had lost his mom and didn't understand it; he probably still doesn't understand it, because how can you really *understand* something like that?

I pat his back. "Bobby," I say. I feel a wetness land against my hand and realize I'm crying, too. "Bobby, I—" A sob escapes from him and reverberates against my chest. "Bobby, I'm *sorry*," I say, and I hold him close for what must be minutes, though not even hours would be enough, really. Not even if I'd been able to hold him through all the years of our childhood would it have been enough. Enough to replace the emptiness Bobby feels.

"Do you have a scar?" Bobby asks. We're crossing the parking lot outside the school. "From that time. You know, that time when I pushed you into the locker and you got that cut?"

I shake my head. "No, why?"

We're walking so close I feel Bobby shrug. "Gooby said so."

"Matt did?" I turn to look at him. His face is still red but probably more from the cold now than anything. "Hm, wonder why."

"Yeah, he said you had a scar, and that if I ever laid a hand on you again, he would get his dad to call my dad."

"Ha!" I try to picture it. Mega laid-back Landon or high-strung Ron. Either one of them speaking on the phone to Tim Handel seems like the setup for some kind of comedy skit. "Wonder which one," I say.

Bobby cracks a smile. The way his lips are chapped at the corners makes me think of the Joker. "What are they like?" he asks. "The Goobys."

I think about that for a second.

"Well, Mr. Landon is super chill, and he has this awesome scraggly beard. And Mr. Ron—" I remember sitting around the breakfast table with them that morning before they left. "Mr. Ron is a little more uptight, I guess. But he's cool, too. I mean, they have a nice balance between the two of them." I pause. "And Matt's just—"

How do I begin?

My shoe is untied, and I stop to tie it, setting my newly tattered copy of *On the Road* down beside me.

"Sorry," I say, "I just gotta tie this." I fiddle with the laces, my fingers all pink and cramped from the cold. "Gosh, it's hard to do when it's this freezing out."

Bobby stops a couple steps ahead of me and turns. He eyes the book for a second, then tilts his head up to look at the night sky. The moonlight catches in his breath. "I'm sorry about your book," he says.

With some effort, I pull the knot tight on my shoe. "Oh, psh." I stand up. "It's all right."

"I could buy you a new one, you know. I'll—"

I catch up to him and we start walking again. "Really, it's not a big deal."

"But I'd kinda like to, if you'd let me."

"Sorry," I say, shaking my head. "But this copy's special."

Bobby stands still, and I turn to face him. He slides his hands into his pockets. "Well, now I feel *really* bad," he says.

"*No!*" I swat the air with my hand. "No, no, it's *special* because now I have a memory to go with it."

He squints his eyes at me, unsure. And then I laugh. "I mean, it's the memory of the night we became friends."

He takes his hands out of his pockets and looks up again. Then he crosses his arms. "True," he says. And we don't say anything else until we reach the parking lot of Yarborough Antiques some minutes later.

"Well," I tell him, "I go this way." I swing my head toward home.

"All right," he says. "I guess I'll see you in a couple days."

"Ugh. That soon? Man, where did this winter break go?"

Bobby shrugs. "It sure as hell beats me." He looks back up Barrow Street, all the Christmas lights still up and illuminating every storefront. It doesn't matter that it's dark out, really. Barrow Street is still light as day.

"It seems like they leave these lights on longer and longer every year," I say. "I mean, New Year's is over, for crying out loud."

"Yeah," Bobby says. "I always miss it, though, when they take it all down."

I follow his gaze all the way to the courthouse lawn. The light from the big Christmas tree leaves the William Griggers statue in shadow. *The brave shall know nothing of death.*

I clear my throat. "Yeah, me, too," I tell Bobby.

twenty-four

On the last day of winter break, I'm sitting in my room. I want to listen to "Anything Could Happen" again, but for some reason Joe's CD keeps skipping. It's like it has a scratch on it or something, which is impossible. I've guarded that thing with my life.

I've already finished *On the Road*, too, so I don't have that anymore. I decide that I like that book a lot. I especially like the way it ends, with the line, *I think of Dean Moriarty, I think of Dean Moriarty, I think of Dean Moriarty.* I love the way it sounds in my head.

So here I am, sitting in my room on the last day of winter break, and for the first time ever in my life I am trying to write. I am trying to keep a journal, since I got the nice one from Joe at Christmas.

I start out, *Well, it's been one heck of a winter break.* Then Mom calls up the stairs. "Hey, Tretch!"

"Yeah?"

"Whatcha doin'?"

"I was just trying out that journal I got for Christmas."

"Oh, okay."

There's a beat.

"Well, you want to ride to Target?"

"Uh-huh," I say. The last time I rode to Target, it was to pick her Christmas gift. The last time I rode to Target, I came out to Joe.

I look at the words I've written on the page. Pretty boring sentence, really. Not exactly how I want to start. "Just give me a second." I take the pen and scribble it out. Then I think for a while, just staring at the page, until finally Mom calls, "Tretch? Still coming?"

"Yes, ma'am," I say. Then I decide.

I think of Matt Gooby, I write, *I think of Matt Gooby, I think of Matt Gooby.* After that, I add, *But I don't think about him as much anymore.*

I drop my pen next to the notebook and swing my legs off

the bed. Mom is at the foot of the stairs. She has her purse and the car keys, ready to go.

"We takin' the highway?" I ask.

"Mm, I thought we'd back-road it."

I smile. "Nice."

At Target, Mom goes to do returns, and I find myself in the CD aisle. I have a ten-dollar bill in my wallet and a little loose change in my pocket. The Ellie Goulding CD is only $9.99—an album called *Halcyon*. I check the back cover. "Anything Could Happen" is song number three.

"*Halcyon*," I read aloud.

The total cost is $10.69. I have exactly $10.75, so I'm in the clear. I work on the plastic wrap while Mom drives us home. She swapped the *Charlie's Angels* DVD box set Joe and I got her for Christmas for store credit. Now she has a brand-new orange sweater, which, I have to say, looks a lot better than the Pepto-Bismol turtleneck she usually wears.

"What's *Halcyon*?" I ask her, through a mouthful of plastic wrap.

"Hmm?" We stop at a red light, and she reaches into her pocket to pull out her iPhone in its bright purple case. "Look it up on here." I'm basically a pro at using the iPhone to search for things at this point. I punch the keypad and enter the words *halcyon definition* into the search bar.

What comes up is this:

halcyon: (adj.) calm, peaceful; rich, wealthy;

happy, joyful (n.) a mythical bird that breeds in

the wintertime, in a nest that floats on the sea

The second part of the definition is highlighted in blue, which means I can click on it if I want. I press the screen with my thumb, and the page disappears for a second. When it reappears, it has a picture of the halcyon bird on it.

"'Breeds in wintertime, in a nest that floats on the sea,'" I read aloud.

"What?"

I give Mom the full definition.

"Hm," she says. "Good winter word."

"Yeah," I agree. "Good winter word." I turn my head to the side and watch her. She stares ahead, bouncing her thumbs on the steering wheel, humming along to the Taylor Swift song playing through the speakers. For a split second, I think about telling her. I think about telling her—

"I have a dance to this song," I say.

"*Really?*" Mom looks surprised.

"Mhmm." I watch the expression change on her face. Something like confusion fading away to a smile, then a laugh.

"So Matt and Lana weren't kidding? You really *do* have the moves?"

"Oh yeah, Mom," I say. "I got the moves." Then I shrug

my shoulders and bob my head. For about twenty seconds, I'm a passenger seat Michael Jackson. Mom continues to tap the beat against the steering wheel, laughing so hard that tears form at the corners of her eyes, and she has to wipe them away.

Sitting on the floor next to the stereo, I take out the old burned CD and replace it with the *Halcyon* one. I sprawl out and listen from song number one all the way to song number thirteen. Then I start it all over again.

It turns out "Anything Could Happen" is only a *taste* of the magic of Ellie Goulding.

Outside, the sky is growing dark. I'm on song number six for the second time when Joe sticks his head in. "I dig this," he says.

I nod. I'm up and moving around, my shoulders bobbing, my arms waving. "It's *Halcyon*," I say. "It's amaaaazing."

Joe smiles. "Well, I hate to break up the party, but Mom says it's time for dinner."

"*Sweet!*" I say. "Give me a minute. I'm just going to finish this song." I shut my eyes and spin. I hear Joe laugh, but when I open my eyes back up, he's gone, and it's just me and my tunes again, in my room. *Me and my tunes and my moves*, I think. I strain my ears for the chorus, this one a lot different than the chorus on "Anything Could Happen." On this one, instead of just a bunch of *eeh-eeh-eeh*s, Ellie repeats a single sentence. "*It's gonna be better,*" she sings, again and again.

"*It's gonna be better, it's gonna be better, it's gonna be better . . .*"

And you know something?

I believe her.

I believe things are going to get better for me, even though sometimes it's hard to. Even though if I shut my eyes and try *so hard* to picture it, sometimes I can't.

But the thing is, if things are really going to get better, then that's great.

Because, right now, dancing in my room by myself, knowing I've got a whole life folding out ahead of me, with a million things to learn from it, I can feel only one thing.

Things are already good.

They really are.

They really, really are.

acknowledgments

So much love and thanks to Sabrina Orah Mark and Reg McKnight, who found the heart of this book first; Laurel Snyder, who taught me about fevers; and Alex Reubert, who started it all with a talk.

Janet Geddis, Rachel Watkins, Frankie Brown, and Nick Simmons, you are my favorites and the heart and soul of the greatest place on earth: Avid Bookshop. Thank you guys so much. To all of our customers, thank you!

David Levithan, my editor, my friend, my reader, my hero, you are the one who said, "It'll all be all right," before we ever even spoke. Your books are the reason books like mine exist, and your belief in this story has meant the world. To everyone at Scholastic, for all of your hard work and devotion, I am so grateful.

Pete Knapp, for your dedication, your kindness, your friendship, and your quiche, I am forever indebted. Jacob Graham, Nick Eliopulos, Andrew Harwell, Jeremy West, and Jeffrey West, thank you all for witnessing. To everyone at the Park Literary Group, I am so thankful for your care.

To Tyler Foy, Rachel Kaplan, Taylor Lear, Rainey Lynch, Hope Hilton, Deirdre Sugiuchi, Beth Thrasher, Anne McLeod, Jenny Wares, Amy Ingalls, Leah Isbell, and Helene Halstead, thank you all for the early encouragements. To my friends—Cleve, Matt, Brian, Nikki, Steven, Natalie, Phil, Ryan, Erin, Graham, and Laura—*thank you.*

To Granddad, who taught me to work hard; to Grandma, who taught me kindness; to Nana, who taught me to read; to Pop, the greatest storyteller; to my dad, who taught me bravery; to my mom, who taught me strength; to my brother, Ben, who is everything true; to my sister, McKinley, who is everything good—I love you all so much more than should be containable by one person.

And to Tyler Goodson, well, here's to the big one. Thank you.